I0545794

The story, all names, characters, and incidents portrayed in this production are fictitious. No identification with actual persons (living or deceased) is intended or should be inferred.

Copyright © 2025 by M.P. Hendy

First paperback edition: July 2025

Book cover by Flux-1

ISBN   978-1-9680275-7-5 (6x9 paperback)
ISBN   978-1-9680275-8-2 (6x9 hardback)

The Survivor's Apocalypse

Part III

The Renado Covenant

M. P. Hendy

Table of Contents

Chapter 25:

The Bullet's Secret Tale

The world outside the Beast was a meaningless, high-speed blur. Inside, it was a universe of focused terror. Kyle's vision tunneled, the edges darkening as the pain in his shoulder radiated in sickening waves. Scott's words, "I don't feel a pulse," replayed on a merciless loop in his skull, each repetition a fresh stab of guilt. He floored the accelerator, the propane-fueled engine screaming in protest as he pushed it far beyond any sensible limit.

In the back, Mike fumbled with a roll of gauze, his hands shaking so badly he could barely wrap it around Kyle's bicep. Tears streamed down his face, mixing with the sweat beading on his brow. "Dad... Dad, she's not..." he choked out, his eyes fixed on the horrifyingly still form of Grace.

"I know, son! Just hold on!" Scott snarled, not at Mike, but at the situation, at the universe. He ripped Grace's body armor further open, exposing the bloody ruin of her shoulder. With grim determination, he shoved the hemostatic gauze into the wound, his knuckles slick with her blood. Her seat was leaned back, but it wasn't enough. "Kyle, I need to start compressions! It's our only shot!"

The command sliced through Mike's grief-stricken panic, replacing it with a surge of desperate adrenaline. Without a second thought, he ripped at the buckles of his own plate carrier, shrugging the heavy armor off and letting it fall to the floor of the car with a muffled thud. The space was impossibly tight, reeking of blood, sweat, and the faint, clean smell of propane exhaust. He scrambled forward, clambering awkwardly over the center console, his knee bumping the gear shift.

He squeezed himself between the two front seats, settling onto Grace's lap, his weight feeling like a profane violation on her still body. "Get her armor off!" Scott barked, his voice a raw command from behind Grace's seat. Mike's fingers found the quick-release tabs on her carrier. He'd seen Junior drill this a hundred times. One sharp tug, and the front panel came loose. Another, and the shoulder straps gave way. He wrestled the heavy carrier off her, the ceramic plates making it a clumsy, dead weight. He tossed it into the back.

Bracing his back against the dashboard, Mike laced his fingers together, placing the heel of his hand on the center of Grace's chest, right over her sternum. He remembered the training, David's calm voice echoing from a distant, safer time. Lock your elbows. Use your body weight. One-and-two-and-three…

He began to push, the rhythmic pressure a stark, violent counterpoint to the car's jarring motion. "One-and-two-and-three-and-four…" he muttered, his voice cracking, tears still flowing freely down his cheeks. He pushed down, feeling the faint, terrifying give of her ribs, praying he wasn't breaking them, praying it was enough.

As Mike worked, Scott shimmied forward, pressing himself into the space directly behind Kyle's seat. "Keep driving, Kyle. Don't you dare slow down," he ordered, his tone leaving no room for argument. He grabbed the roll of gauze Mike had dropped, expertly wrapping it around Kyle's shoulder, pulling it tight over the entry wound above his scapula and then crossbody to the exit wound below his clavicle. The pressure was intense, forcing a strangled gasp from Kyle. "I got it… I got it," Kyle grunted, his knuckles white on the steering wheel. Every push Mike gave to Grace's chest felt like a hammer blow to his own soul. His fault. This was his fault.

On the northern hillside overlooking the ranch. Seth lay prone in the tall, sun-scorched grass, a pair of binoculars pressed to his eyes, scanning the distant highway. Beside him, Noah was a study in stillness, his high-caliber sniper rifle resting on its bipod, its scope glinting. It was a routine watch, a familiar rhythm of silence and observation.

Then, a sound cut through the drone of cicadas. Faint at first, it grew rapidly into the distinctive, violent whistle of a turbocharger spooling to its limit. Seth lowered his binoculars, frowning. He knew that sound. It was Aidan's Beast, but it was wrong. Angry. Desperate. "Noah," Seth said, his voice tight. "That's Aidan's car. Whoever's driving… they're pushing it way too hard."

Noah, without moving his head, was already reaching for the radio on his belt. The car crested a distant rise, a flash of red metal kicking up a massive plume of dust. It wasn't driving; it was racing. "David, Aidan, this is Noah on North Hill," he spoke, his voice calm and clipped. "Beast is inbound, north road. Coming in hot. Looks like a critical emergency. Recommend immediate medical standby at the garage.

Prepare for the worst." A beat of static, then David's voice, devoid of panic, resonating with grim authority. "Copy, Noah. Andrea to the garage, now. Medical emergency. Junior, get down here. Aidan, open the garage door."

The high-pitched whine of the turbocharger died with an abrupt cough as The Beast skidded to a halt on the gravel in front of the garage, its red paint now caked in a thick layer of pale Texas dust. The rear passenger door flew open before the car had even fully stopped, and Scott stumbled out, his face a mask of grim determination, his AR-15 held at a low ready. Blood soaked the sleeve of his right arm, but he ignored it.

The real horror unfolded as Junior and Brian wrenched open the driver's side door. Kyle slumped against the frame, his face ashen, a dark, blossoming stain spreading across the front of his body armor, just below his right collarbone. But his eyes weren't on his own injury. They were locked on the passenger seat.

It was a scene of frantic, desperate tragedy. Mike, Scott's fourteen-year-old son, was half-sprawled over Grace's still form. His face was tear-streaked, his hands pressed rhythmically against her sternum, his small frame pumping with a strength born of pure terror. "She's not breathing!" he screamed, his voice cracking with panic. "I felt her pulse go... it's gone! I can't stop!"

"Move!" Andrea's voice cut through the noise like a scalpel, sharp and commanding. She was already at the passenger door, Olivia and Sophia right behind her with the gurney. "Mike, son, you did good. You did real good. Now let me have her." Junior pushed past Andrea and carefully lifted Grace out of the car. Her body armor had clearly been shed by Mike in his desperate CPR attempt, leaving her vulnerable and painfully light in Junior's arms. He laid her gently, almost reverently, onto the gurney.

Brian and Caleb, grim-faced, already had Kyle by the arms, helping him to the aid station in the garage. Kyle, though pale, was still conscious, muttering something about Grace. As Olivia took over CPR on Grace, Andrea turned sharply to Scott. "What happened?" she demanded, her gaze sweeping over the gurney to her husband's bloodied arm. Scott, his voice clipped and strained, gasped out the terrifying truth. "A shooter. Beyond the East ridge... shot through Kyle's shoulder, missed his armor. Bullet went into Grace's left shoulder." His voice broke. "I think she's gone. I couldn't feel a pulse."

As Scott uttered the words, Nicole, who was standing on the west side of the porch, let out a guttural shriek that tore through the stifling heat of the late afternoon. Her legs gave out, and she crumpled to the floor, a desperate, raw sound escaping her lips. Her daughter. Her sweet Grace. The world spun around her, blurring into a kaleidoscope of green grass, the red gleam of Aidan's car, and the horrifying image of the gurney being wheeled away.

Mike, still kneeling in the driveway where he stopped, stared blankly at his own blood-stained hands, tears streaming silently down his face, a silent testament to the terror that had just gripped him. He didn't register the screaming or the orders being given around him, only the cold, empty dread in his stomach.

Andrea, however, had no time for the luxury of despair. Her nurse's instinct, honed by years of crisis, superseded personal grief. She leaned over Grace, her fingers flying to the girl's neck, then her wrist. Nothing. A flicker of panic, cold and sharp, threatened to pierce her professional facade. But then, as Olivia continued the steady compressions, Andrea's ear pressed against Grace's lips. A whisper. A ghost of a whisper. An almost imperceptible wisp of warm air.

"Hold compressions!" Andrea snapped, her voice suddenly electrifying the air. Everyone froze, their eyes fixed on her. She pressed her ear harder against Grace's chest, her fingers searching for a pulse again, this time with a laser-like focus. A tremor. Faint, thready, but undeniably there. A pulse! "She's alive!" Andrea's voice was a guttural shout of triumph and pure, unadulterated relief. "Barely, but she's alive! Get her inside! Now!"

From the porch, David's gaze was a steel instrument, methodically parsing the scene. He saw Nicole, now being helped to her feet by a stunned but steady Summer, her sobs devolving into ragged, tearing gasps. He saw Mike, a statue of grief in the driveway, his son's friend, paralyzed by the horror he'd witnessed. His eyes tracked the gurney's path, then settled on Scott, who had risen to his full height, his face grim, his posture that of a soldier waiting for debriefing. Finally, he looked at the Beast, its crimson paint spattered with mud and covered in dust. The engine ticked softly as it cooled, the only sound in the sudden, still silence.

David raised the radio to his lips, his voice a low, calm counterpoint to the chaos. "Seth, status." The reply was immediate, crackling with perfect clarity. Seth's young voice was devoid of panic, a testament to his training. "Negative, Dad. We have eyes on the north road for three miles in both directions. The Beast wasn't followed. The surrounding area is clear."

"Good. Maintain overwatch," David commanded. "Tiffany, report to the aid station immediately. Andrea needs you. Acknowledge." "Acknowledged, David. On my way," Tiffany's voice came back, solid and dependable. "Lily, Josh. Grab Brian and Caleb. Unload the cargo from the Beast. Full quarantine protocol. Get the sow and piglets to the smithy. I want them secured and fed within thirty minutes." "Copy that, Daddy," Lily's voice confirmed.

With the ranch's external security confirmed and its internal assets mobilized, David descended the porch steps. The oppressive Texas heat seemed to bend around him, recoiling from the cold focus in his eyes. He bypassed Nicole, knowing he was in no position to console, and walked directly to Mike. He placed a heavy, grounding hand on the boy's trembling shoulder.

The weight of David's hand was an anchor in the swirling chaos of Mike's mind. The boy's breath hitched, a dry, rattling sob. He finally tore his eyes away from the blood stains on his palms. He looked up into David's face, a face

9

that held no judgment, no panic, only an unnerving, absolute calm.

"Mike," David's voice was low, cutting through the boy's internal screaming. "Look at me." Mike blinked, trying to focus. The world swam in a haze of heat and horror. "I need you to listen to me very carefully," David continued, his grip firm but not painful. "You're going to walk into the main house. You're going to go to the kitchen sink. You will wash your hands and face. Then you will sit at the table and wait for me. Do you understand?"

The instructions were simple, a lifeline of concrete tasks. Mike could only manage a jerky, spastic nod, his throat too tight for words. "Go now," David said, giving his shoulder a final, grounding squeeze before releasing him. He watched for a moment as the boy, moving like a sleepwalker, stumbled towards the porch steps, a puppet whose strings had just been reattached.

With Mike on his way, David pivoted, his stride long and purposeful as he crossed the driveway towards the cavernous opening of the garage. The scent of ozone from the Beast's hot engine mingled with the sharper, more metallic smell of blood and antiseptic. Inside, Kyle sat shirtless on a stool, his back ramrod straight as Tiffany worked with grim efficiency on his shoulder. The entry wound on his back was already cleaned and covered, but the exit wound below his collarbone was a ragged, angry mess. Tiffany was carefully applying a pressure dressing.

Kyle's jaw was a knot of granite. His eyes, burning with a mixture of pain and self-recrimination, locked onto

David's as he approached. "David, I…" he began, his voice a gravelly rasp. "It came out of nowhere. A single shot from the tree line. I didn't even see…" "Later, Kyle," David interrupted, his tone leaving no room for argument. He stopped before him, his gaze sweeping over Tiffany's handiwork, then meeting Kyle's. "Your report can wait. Your only job right now is to let Tiffany fix you. Then you get stitched, get some water, and get some rest." "But Grace—I have to…"

"I will handle Grace," David stated, the words carrying the finality of a closing vault door. He placed a hand on Kyle's good shoulder, forcing the man's tense frame to relax fractionally. "I'll take care of everything. You just focus on healing. That's an order." Kyle looked like he wanted to argue, to do something, but he finally deflated, giving a tight, pained nod. David met Tiffany's eyes over Kyle's head, a silent exchange of understanding passing between them.

The aid station was a pocket of sterile chill and focused tension. The quiet hum of the medical monitors was the only sound. Andrea, her face pale and set, stood beside a medical bed. On it lay Grace, looking terrifyingly small and still. An IV line ran into her arm, and a clear plastic tube protruded from the side of her chest, draining into a canister on the floor. The fluid inside was a sickening dark red.

David came to a stop beside Andrea, his eyes taking in every detail with a cold, diagnostic precision: Grace's waxy pallor, the shallow, mechanically assisted rise and fall of her chest, the worryingly slow drip in the IV bag. "Andrea. Report," he said, his voice quiet but demanding.

Andrea didn't look at him, her attention glued to the monitor displaying Grace's vitals. "Tension pneumothorax. Her left lung completely collapsed. I've inserted a thoracostomy tube to re-inflate it, but she's drowning in her own blood. Massive hemothorax." She finally turned to face him, her professional mask firmly in place, but her eyes betrayed the tremor in her hands. "The bullet is still in her. It passed clean through Kyle, and entered her upper left chest. It's lodged against the inside of her fourth rib, probably right next to the pericardium. Her pulse is thready, blood pressure is dangerously low."

David processed the information, his mind a silent, whirring engine of calculation and consequence. He had seen every permutation of battlefield trauma. He knew what she was saying, and what she was leaving unsaid. "We need to get the bullet out," David stated, his voice a low command that cut through the sterile air. "It's putting pressure on the pericardium and contributing to the bleeding. Can we do it from the front?"

Andrea's gaze flickered from the monitor to David, then to Grace's chest. "Maybe," she conceded, her voice tight with professional caution. "If it's just lodged against the rib and hasn't fragmented or embedded itself in the bone, I might be able to retrieve it with forceps through a small incision. But if it shattered... David, if there are fragments, I don't have the equipment or the skill for that kind of delicate surgery. We'd be doing more harm than good."

"It didn't fragment," David said with absolute certainty. He gestured vaguely toward the garage, where Kyle was being treated. "It went through Kyle first. Fourteen-plus inches of muscle, fascia, and tissue. It was moving slow by the time it hit her. It will be flattened, maybe slightly deformed, but intact." His intelligence wasn't just knowledge; it was a profound, almost supernatural understanding of cause and effect, of physics and biology intertwining in a bloody dance.

Andrea chewed on her lower lip, considering his words. It made a grim kind of sense. She gave a short, decisive nod. "Alright. But she's lost a lot of blood. Her pressure won't sustain any procedure, no matter how minor. We need O positive blood." Without another word, David keyed his radio. His voice boomed with calm authority. "Net call, net call, net call, all stations. This is David. Any volunteer with O Positive blood type, report to the aid station in the main house immediately. I say again, all O Positive donors, report to the aid station now. David out."

Just as the radio crackled into silence, the door to the aid station slid open. Tiffany stepped inside, her face etched with concern but her movements steady. She had just finished cleaning and dressing Kyle's wounds, stabilizing him for the long healing process ahead. She took in the scene, David at the radio, Andrea prepping a surgical tray, and Grace looking so fragile on the bed, and her maternal instincts flared.

"He's stable," she reported quietly to David, her eyes fixed on Grace. "Just a clean through-and-through. He'll be fine. What do you need?" "Help Andrea," David said, his focus already back on his daughter. "We're taking the bullet out. And get ready for transfusions. I've put out the call." Tiffany nodded, shedding her outer layer and immediately moving to the sink to scrub in, a seamless part of the life-saving machine David was assembling.

Outside, the oppressive Texas heat baked the concrete of the driveway. Aidan's pride and joy, 'The Beast', sat gleaming red under the afternoon sun, its powerful engine finally cool. Josh and Lily approached, their task to unload the captured pigs and get them settled into the quarantine smithy. "Thing sounds mean," Josh commented, pulling on a pair of thick work gloves.

Lily offered a slight smile, pulling open the heavy front passenger door to retrieve the empty water bottles. The moment the door swung wide, the smell hit her, the hot, coppery tang of blood, thick and overwhelming. Her eyes dropped to the seat. The black upholstery was saturated with a dark, crusting stain that spread across the cushion and down the side. A small pool of it had collected on the floor mat. Josh saw it a second later. "Whoa, looks like Kyle bled more than we thought…"

But Lily wasn't looking at the main stain anymore. Her gaze was cataloging the scene with a horrifying clarity. Her heart began to pound a frantic, heavy rhythm against her ribs. Beside the bloodstain rested the back plate from an armor carrier. It was smaller than Kyle's. And lying half on the floor, half-propped against the transmission tunnel, was Junior's custom AR-10. Not Kyle's AR-15. Junior's rifle. The one he'd given to Grace for this trip.

The pieces clicked together in Lily's mind with the sickening finality of a chambered round. "Lily?" Josh asked, his brow furrowed in confusion as he watched the color drain

14

from her face. "You alright?" She didn't answer. The sheer volume of blood... this wasn't a clean wound. This was catastrophic. "No..." The word was a choked gasp, a whisper of air stolen from her lungs. She saw her sister's sweet, observant face, her shy smile. She saw Grace.

"Lily, what is it?" Josh took a step toward her, his concern turning to alarm. "Josh..." Her voice cracked, failing her. "That's not... it's not Kyle's blood." Her eyes locked on the armor plate. The strength evaporated from her legs. A strangled sob tore from her throat as her knees buckled. She collapsed onto the hot concrete of the driveway, the rough surface scraping her hands as she caught herself. "Whoa, hey!" Josh rushed forward, dropping to one knee beside her, his hands hovering, unsure where to touch. "Lily! Talk to me! What's wrong? What do you mean it's not Kyle's?"

Tears streamed down her face, mixing with the dust on her cheeks. She couldn't form a coherent thought, couldn't voice the nightmare scenario playing out in her head. She could only shake her head, her body wracked with tremors, and point a trembling finger at the car's interior. "It... It was Grace."

That night, Nicole was a crumpled form on the largest sofa, her body shuddering with each silent cry. Summer had an arm wrapped tightly around her, while Tiffany sat beside them, her hands clutched together. Not far away, Lily was curled into Josh's side, her face buried in his shoulder. Her earlier, frantic collapse had subsided into a state of trembling shock. Josh held her fast, his jaw set like stone. Across the room, Callie, her usual humor completely extinguished, wiped at her eyes with the back of her hand, her gaze fixed on the floor. And near the doorway, leaning against Andrea's chair, as if he couldn't trust his own legs, was Scott.

At the center of it all stood David. He was positioned by the cold fireplace, a solitary pillar of unnatural calm. His posture was straight, his face impassive. But his wives knew. Jennifer, her playful nature replaced by a grim watchfulness, saw the micro-tightening around his eyes. Jessica, who could read him better than any book, saw the rigid set of his shoulders, the unyielding control he was exerting over a volcano of rage. Elena noted the stillness of his hands and knew it was the most dangerous sign of all. He was a predator coiled to strike, and the entire ranch was his den. "Andrea. Report."

Andrea, sitting in an armchair next to her husband Scott standing behind her, looked up. The nurse was pale with exhaustion, her eyes shadowed. "The bullet," she said, her voice clinical but strained. "It entered her left shoulder, high. It scraped the bone, but it tore through the upper lobe of her left lung before lodging against the interior of her rib. There was... significant internal bleeding. I've repaired the lung as best I can and stopped the bleed. She's stable, for now." She took a shaky breath. "But she lost a lot of blood. Seth is with her now, giving a direct transfusion. We have a lot of doners here. She's still unconscious. The next 48 hours are critical."

A fresh wave of muffled sobs broke from Nicole. David's eyes softened for a fraction of a second as he looked at her. "Kyle?" David's voice was clipped, moving on. "The bullet passed clean through his shoulder muscle," Andrea continued. "It's a nasty wound, but it missed the artery and the bone. I've cleaned it and stitched it. He's on heavy painkillers and resting in the guest room next door. He's lucky. Incredibly lucky." The unspoken implication hung in the air: Grace wasn't.

David nodded slowly, then reached into the pocket of his jeans. The gesture was deliberate, drawing every eye in the room. He opened his palm, and resting in the center was the misshapen piece of copper he'd taken from Andrea. It was dull, ugly, and stained with his daughter's blood.

His gaze, cold and hard as forged steel, moved from the bullet. He didn't want to discuss the attack yet. Instead, his eyes swept the room, cataloging, assessing. They landed on Josh. "Josh," David's voice was unnervingly level, cutting through the emotional fog. "Report." Josh straightened. "Sir. The sow and seven piglets are secure in the Smithy. Junior and Caleb helped Lily and me get them settled. They're awake from their sedation and are feeding. The building is locked down."

"Good." A single, clipped word of approval. David's attention shifted, his head turning slightly to find his eldest son, Aidan, who was leaning against the far wall, arms crossed. The faint smell of soap and degreaser clung to him. "Aidan. The Beast." Aidan pushed off the wall. "Hosed out, inside and out. Scrubbed the seats where… where Grace and Kyle were." He hesitated for a fraction of a second, the only crack in his composure. "Blood's gone. It's sitting by the garage with the doors open, airing out. It'll be dry and ready for service by morning."

David nodded again. His gaze found Scott, who stood protectively behind Andrea's chair, one hand resting on her shoulder. "Scott. How's Mike?" Scott swallowed hard, his face pale and drawn. He looked a decade older than he had this morning. "Mike's... he's shook up bad, David. He's resting now. He, uh... he keeps asking about Grace. He doesn't understand why she isn't awake yet." His voice cracked at her name. "Andrea gave him something to help him sleep. He's tough, but... he's just a kid."

A flicker of something, empathy, maybe pain, crossed David's features as he looked at Andrea. "You've done well, Andrea. Get some rest when you can. Kayla will coordinate the blood donations." Andrea just nodded, too exhausted to speak. Finally, David's eyes settled on Junior, who stood near the doorway to the main hall. "Junior." "Sir," Junior responded instantly, his voice low and clear, cutting through the stagnant air.

With a practiced, fluid motion, David tossed the object from his palm. It spun through the air, an ugly little piece of copper-jacketed lead, catching the light as it flew. Junior's hand shot out, snatching it from the air. The muffled thump as it landed in his palm was the loudest sound in the room. "Tell me what you see," David commanded, his voice dropping into a register that demanded absolute focus.

The entire room seemed to lean in. Elena watched David, her expression a mixture of fear and fascination, captivated by the cold, brilliant mind she'd fallen for. Jennifer, standing a few feet from David, saw the unyielding authority, the Master taking command, and felt a shiver of familiar response. Jessica, closest of all, watched her Daddy work, her sassy demeanor for once completely absent, replaced by a fierce, trusting loyalty.

Junior didn't answer immediately. He rolled the deformed bullet between his thumb and forefinger, his head tilted. His other hand came up to support it as he examined the base, the slight mushrooming of the tip, the distinct grooves carved into its side by the rifle's barrel.

"It's a .30 caliber," he began, his voice methodical, the gunsmith taking over from the son. "124 grain, give or take, accounting for the deformation. Copper jacketed, but with a bit of oxidation." He looked up, his eyes meeting David's. "The weight is too light for a .308 Winchester or a .30-06. Those are typically 150 grains or heavier. This is almost certainly a 7.62 by 39 millimeter."

A low murmur rippled through the room. It wasn't a hunter's round. It was a soldier's. "Which means the firearm was most likely an AK platform, an AK-47 or one of its countless variants, or an SKS," Junior continued, his gaze drifting to Noah. "The rifling marks are consistent with common Combloc barrels. It's cheap, mass-produced ammunition. Steel-cased, most likely. The kind you buy in bulk tins. This wasn't a precision shooter with a custom rifle. This was someone with a common, rugged, reliable weapon."

He paused, turning the bullet over one last time. "They were close. Maybe a hundred, hundred-fifty yards. The bullet didn't tumble; it was still stable when it hit Kyle. That's why it had enough energy left to pass through his shoulder and still do so much damage to Grace." The analysis hung in the air, cold, clinical, and terrifying. They weren't dealing with a lone, desperate hunter. They were dealing with someone armed for a fight.

David absorbed the information, his expression unchanging. It was exactly what he suspected, but he needed the physical confirmation. He needed his people to hear it from their expert. "Junior," he said, his voice a low, steady rumble that cut through the silence. "Given the commonality of the weapon and ammunition, how difficult would it be to identify the person who fired this shot? What are we looking for?"

Junior placed the bullet on the table, his expression professional yet grim. "Extremely difficult, Dad. An AK platform... it's the cockroach of the rifle world. It's everywhere. Millions were made. The ammunition is just as common. There's no unique signature here. We're not looking for a needle in a haystack; we're looking for a specific piece of straw." He ran a hand through his hair. "But I don't think the 'who' is as important as the 'why' right now. And I have a theory on that."

Chapter 26:

The Patriarch's Wrath

The entire room waited in silence for Junior to continue. But before he could, Scott spoke up, his voice rough and strained. "Maybe it's simpler than all that, Junior," he said, looking around the room, desperate for agreement. "We were out in the open, makin' noise, settin' that big trap. Maybe some other fella was hunting the same area. Saw us, panicked, and took a potshot before running off. Could have just been after the same damn pigs we were."

It was a comforting thought, a return to the familiar threat of desperate but disorganized survivors. David, however, saw the flaw immediately. He turned his steady, deep-set eyes toward Scott. "If they wanted pork, Scott, why did they shoot? You said yourself there were still two full-grown hogs and at least eight piglets there. If all they wanted was food, they could have waited for you to leave and taken the rest. A single shot would've scared the pigs, or worse, started a firefight."

The simple, logical dismantling of Scott's theory sent a fresh wave of unease through the room. Junior nodded in appreciation of his father's point. "Exactly. The pigs weren't the primary target." He looked from his father to Scott, then let his gaze sweep over the younger women in the room. "My first thought was that Grace was the target. Think about it. Whoever was watching saw a young, healthy girl expertly building and setting a complex trap. They saw skill. They saw potential. In this world, a person like that... she's a prize. A far better prize than pork." A collective sharp intake of breath came from several corners of the room.

"In that scenario," Junior continued, laying out the grim logic, "Kyle was just an obstacle. A big, armed man standing between the shooter and the prize. They fire one shot to take him out of the equation, then move in to grab Grace." He let that horrifying image hang in the air for a moment before shaking his head. "But that doesn't quite fit either. It's cleaner, but it's still not right."

The room held its breath. "Let's re-examine it from the shooter's perspective," Junior began, his voice dropping, taking on the tone of a detective re-creating a crime. "They weren't there for us, not initially. They were moving through the territory, scouting most likely, maybe hunting, like Scott said, but they certainly weren't hunters. Then, they stumble upon our group. They stop, they watch, they assess."

He painted a vivid picture of a predator happening upon unexpected prey. "They see skilled people, working efficiently. But they're not looking to start a war. Then their focus lands on Grace. They see her competence, her expertise. And in that moment, the entire mission changes. The patrol is abandoned, an impulse takes over. A new, far more valuable prize is right there for the taking. It wasn't a long, premeditated plan to find her; it was an opportunistic decision made in a matter of seconds. Grace becomes a target of opportunity."

Having established the motive, Junior laid out the grim mechanics of the execution. "So, they decide, right then and there, to take her. The first step is to eliminate her guardian instantly and silently. They aim for Kyle's head." He paused, letting the weight of the moment settle. "But the rifle is inaccurate, or the shooter flinches under pressure. The shot goes low, hitting Kyle in the shoulder. A disabling, but not instantly fatal, wound." "But the bullet doesn't stop. It passes clean through Kyle... and hits Grace."

He placed the bullet down with chilling finality. "And that's why there was no second shot. That's why they vanished. Not because they were scared. Not because they missed. It's because they accidentally shot the person they wanted to capture." The puzzle pieces clicked into place with an awful, sickening sound. The shooter probably wanted to kill Kyle. But they certainly didn't want to kill Grace. They wanted to take her. The single bullet was a catastrophic failure on their part.

"This person, or this group," Junior stated, his voice now low and dangerous, "have no reservations about taking people. They saw our team, they assessed them, and they picked a target. Whoever they are, they somehow thought they deserved Grace. Now, who or what would give someone that much confidence?"

From her seat beside David, Jessica watched him, not Junior. She saw what no one else did, a detail so subtle it would have been lost on anyone who didn't know him as intimately as she did. His hand, resting on his knee, clenched into a fist so tight his knuckles turned white. And then, a single, swift movement, his hand rising to his face, the side of his index finger brushing just under his eye, discreetly wiping away a single tear before it could betray the storm raging within him. The great patriarch, was fighting a losing battle against the raw, primal fear of a father. His facade of stoic calm was cracking under the unbearable pressure.

Junior turned his fiery gaze from the group to his father. With a flick of his wrist, he tossed the bullet through the air. David caught it reflexively, his hand closing around it. The weight of it seemed to anchor him, to pull all his roiling emotions into a single point of focus. "What do you want to do?" Junior asked. It wasn't just a question; it was the transfer of command. The vanguard had assessed the threat; now the leader had to give the order.

David's eyes, which had been fixed on his closed fist, snapped to Junior. The grief and fear that Jessica had witnessed were gone, burned away and replaced by something harder, colder, and infinitely more terrifying. It was the same temporal strength that flowed through his children, now manifest in its purest, most potent form. "Mobilize volunteers," David's voice was devoid of its usual warmth and wit. It was the voice of a man giving an order of execution. "As many as we can spare."

Nicole, her sweet face pale with worry, leaned forward. "David? What are you going to do?" Tanya, sitting on her side, leaned in, her expression a mirror of Nicole's concern. David didn't look at them. His gaze was still locked with Junior's, a silent understanding passing between father and son. His fingers tightened around the bullet, the lead inside a cold promise against his palm. He finally turned his head, his eyes sweeping over his worried wives, but the cold fury in them was not for them. "I'm going to kill them."

It wasn't a threat. It was a pronouncement of fact, as certain as the sun's rise. For Emma and Callie, the words were a key turning a lock on a room they tried to keep sealed. The air in the ranch vanished, replaced by the cold, metallic scent of blood and fear from the barracks of the Air Force Base. Six months melted away in an instant. They weren't in David's protected fortress anymore; they were back in that hell, watching Junior, his face a mask of primal fury, his voice the same chilling, flat monotone David had just used. Now, seeing that same terrifying resolve in the patriarch, the man whose protection was the bedrock of their new world, was both petrifying and profoundly reassuring.

Callie's bubbly personality evaporated, her face paling as she stared at David, her eyes wide with a familiar terror. Emma's reaction was more visceral. Her breath hitched, and her hand flew instinctively to her throat, her fingers tracing the cool, unyielding metal of the eternity collar she wore. The weight of it was a constant reminder, but in this moment, it was an anchor. David's voice from her collaring ceremony echoed in her mind, clearer than the nervous whispers of the women around her. "Anyone, anyone, who dares to lay a harmful hand upon a woman wearing one of these collars… will face the absolute torment of every soul under this roof."

He hadn't been speaking of his wives, or Junior's. He had been speaking of his family. Grace, his daughter, was certainly under that umbrella of protection. The promise held.

The torment was coming. Emma's gaze, wide and haunted, shot to Junior. There was no surprise on his face. Not a flicker of shock, not a hint of debate. His expression was a placid lake reflecting a stormy sky, outwardly calm, but holding a deep, roiling power beneath the surface. He had become the angel of death that day at the base, and now she saw that he was merely the extension of a much greater, more terrifying will.

Her eyes darted around the room, a desperate search for dissent or disbelief, but she found none. What she found was far more unsettling. A profound, almost religious inevitability had settled over David's wives and children. It was in the way Tiffany straightened her spine, her jaw set not with anger, but with grim resolve. It was in the way Jennifer had a faint smile touch her lips, a look of dark pride and vindication. Jessica, ever his sassy firecracker, simply crossed her arms, a single, sharp nod her only comment. The other wives, Summer, Taylor, Nicole, Elena, Kayla, Tanya, their faces were a tapestry of somber understanding. They were mothers, protectors. One of their own had been grievously wounded, a child of their house. There was no question of the response.

If the wives were the foundation of trust, the children were the sharpened steel. Callie felt a tremor of fear run through her, so profound it made her teeth ache. This wasn't a family discussing revenge. This was a war council finalizing a declaration. The air was thick with unspoken oaths and shared history she couldn't begin to comprehend. These people, bound by blood and a strange, temporal legacy, moved as one entity. Her bubbly personality, her defense mechanism against the horrors of the new world, had not just evaporated; it felt like a foolish, childish costume she'd been stripped of. She saw them now for what they were. They were not just survivors. They were predators. They were the apex of this broken world, and someone had just wounded one of their young. The thought solidified in her mind with terrifying clarity: these people were going to descend upon the region like the armies of death.

Her terrified gaze landed back on Junior. Now, seeing him in the context of his family, she understood he was just one storm front in a much larger hurricane. Her eyes traced over his body, catching on the intricate ink that covered his left arm. She'd seen it before, but in her hero-worship and the chaos of their new life, she had never truly looked at it. Now, she did.

The tattoo was a masterpiece of dark, intricate art. Four horsemen, thundering across a blasted landscape under a sky of fire and shadow. They were terrifying, mythic figures, rendered in stunning, brutal detail. But it was the faces that made Callie's blood run cold. The first horseman, on a white steed, wore a crown and carried a bow. His face, etched with lines of ancient knowledge and unshakeable authority, was David's. Conquest. The second, on a blood-red horse, brandished a great sword, his face a mask of primal fury and martial perfection. It was Junior. War.

The third, on a black horse, held a set of scales, his expression one of cold calculation and logistical certainty. It was Brian, the farmer who fed their world. Famine, or perhaps the control over it. The fourth horseman rode a pale horse, and his face was Aidan's. Behind him, Hell followed. Death.

Callie's breath hitched in a choked sob. It wasn't a homage. It wasn't a bit of edgy art. It was a statement of intent. A family crest. A warning. This was who they were. This was what they did to those who crossed them. They were the cleansing fire. They were the end. The horsemen of the apocalypse were real. And they were family.

Junior turned, his posture straightening as he surveyed the assembled faces. The fiery grief in his eyes had cooled, banked into the focused embers of a combat leader. He didn't need a rousing speech. He didn't need to justify the cause. Grace, lying unconscious and breathing shallowly in the infirmary below their feet, was all the justification they needed. His voice, unlike his father's, wasn't cold. It was raw, a low growl that cut through the silence and vibrated in the chests of everyone present. "Who wants to go?"

The response was immediate, a ripple of movement through the room. Aidan was the first on his feet. "The Beast will be fueled and ready," he said, his voice tight. "And I'll have the other vehicles prepped for a long haul." It wasn't a question of if he was going; it was a statement of his role in the operation.

After several minutes, David's gaze swept across the volunteers. He nodded once, a sharp, definitive motion. "That's three vehicles," he stated, his voice flat and devoid of emotion. "Sixteen people. Junior and myself included." The calculation was made. The sentence was passed.

Junior stepped forward, his eyes scanning the faces of the war party his father had just sanctioned. His voice was a whip crack in the tense air, calling the roll. "Josh, Lily, Darrel, Reagan, Caleb, Seth, Noah, Andrew, Elena, Emma, Riley, Marvin, Parker and Scott." He paused, his gaze meeting each of theirs, forging a silent contract of violence and retribution. "You're with us. Everyone else," he commanded, his voice dropping to a low, serious tone, "is on high alert. You will protect this ranch. Brian, I want our comms locked down and monitored. Andrea, you have command of the infirmary. No one bothers you, you get whatever you need. Understood?"

A chorus of assent answered him. As the group began to break, the quiet energy shifting towards purposeful preparation, Emma moved to Junior's side. She placed a hand on his arm, her touch a familiar anchor in the storm. Olivia and Riley stood close by, their faces a mixture of concern and readiness, a silent trinity of support. "Junior," Emma began, her voice low and for his ears only. "What are the parameters? What is the objective beyond just... finding them?"

The hard lines around Junior's eyes softened as he looked down at her. He cupped her cheek, his thumb stroking her skin, a brief, tender moment that was a world away from the commander he had just been. "The objective is to eliminate the threat," he said softly, the love for her coloring his tone. "Permanently. Grace won't wake up in a world where the person who did this to her is still breathing. We're going to make sure of that. You stay within visual of me or Riley at all times." Emma nodded, her own resolve hardening at his words.

Junior turned back to the larger group, his command presence snapping back into place like a physical shield. "Listen up!" We're likely looking for someone armed with an AK variant, or an SKS. That's our identifier." He let that sink in before delivering the rules of engagement, his voice now ice-cold and laced with venom. "Anyone we find carrying one of those weapon systems is a person of interest. Anyone who raises one of those rifles at you, or at anyone in our family, is a confirmed hostile. You do not wait to be fired upon. You do not ask questions. You end the threat. Am I clear?"

Crystal clear nods came from every member of the party. "Good," Junior said, a muscle working in his jaw. "We start at the attack site. The shooter knows the area, which means they probably live near it. We'll secure the site and begin a systematic sweep, spiraling outwards. House by house, settlement by settlement. We'll be quiet, we'll be thorough, and we will be relentless."

David, who had been observing the briefing, finally rose. "Junior's assessment is sound," he began. "The plan is solid. But vengeance is a dish best served by those who are rested and focused, not running on adrenaline and rage." He scanned the faces of the group. "You have eight hours," David declared. "That puts us at 05:30. I want you fed, hydrated, and with at least six hours of sleep. Check your gear, check it again, and then have your partner check it. We move with the dawn. When we find these people, there will be no hesitation, no quarter. They shot my family. They invited this storm to their door, and we are going to deliver."

He turned to his wives, who were gathered in the kitchen. A faint, affectionate smile touched his lips as he met Jessica's gaze. "Daddy," she purred, stepping forward to adjust the collar of his shirt, "Are you sure six hours is enough? I can think of some… stress-relieving activities that might help you get properly rested." Jennifer, standing beside her, chuckled. "Now Jessica, don't be greedy. Master needs his strength for the hunt." David simply placed a hand on Jessica's waist. "There will be time for celebration when we return," he said, the promise in his voice making her grin. "But not just you. Every single one of you."

Callie watched it all, her normally bubbly personality feeling flattened and out of place. She felt like a shaken soda can in a library. Just yesterday, she'd been joking with Grace, planning out her infiltration into Junior's bed. Now, Grace was unconscious, fighting for her life, and the entire ranch was transforming into a military staging ground. Junior was in the center of it all, his handsome face a mask of professional calm as he conferred with his wives. He was a part of this storm David had promised to deliver.

Her eyes, however, kept drifting away from the kinetic energy of the war party and landing on the still point in the room: Lynn. The older woman stood near the arched entryway to the dining room, her arms crossed tightly over her chest. She wasn't preparing gear or speaking in hushed tones. She was just watching, her expression a complex tapestry of weary resignation and something else… something that looked unnervingly like memory.

While Jessica and Jennifer's playful-yet-serious exchange with David was a dynamic Callie was still getting used to, Lynn's stillness felt profound. She was a veteran of a different kind of war, the one that happened in the terrifying moments when David's calm, patriarchal leadership was stripped away to reveal the warlord beneath. Callie needed to understand. She needed perspective from someone who wasn't caught up in the immediate family drama or the battle-ready adrenaline.

Taking a steadying breath, she pushed off the wall and navigated the organized chaos, her sneakers silent on the hardwood floor. "Lynn?" she said softly as she approached. The older woman's eyes shifted from the war party to Callie. They were tired eyes, but sharp. "Callie. You should be trying to get some sleep. It's going to be a long night, and an even longer few days." "I can't," Callie admitted, wringing her hands. "My brain feels like it's full of bees. I keep seeing... I just..." She gestured vaguely towards the armed-to-the-teeth group. "Do you have any idea what's going to happen? I mean, really happen?"

Lynn's gaze drifted back to David, and a humorless, tight smile touched her lips for a fraction of a second. It was the saddest smile Callie had ever seen. "Oh, I have a very good idea," Lynn said, her voice low and gravelly, meant only for Callie. "A lot of people are going to die. And they aren't going to be our people."

Callie's blood ran cold. "How can you be so sure?" "Because David never, ever does anything halfway," Lynn stated, as if it were an immutable law of physics. She turned her body slightly, creating a small pocket of privacy for them in the bustling room. "The day he found me, I was on my way here, but I got a flat tire. I thought it was just bad luck. When he finally found me, three men came out. They weren't there to wish us well."

Callie swallowed hard, picturing it. "I thought we were dead," Lynn continued, her eyes unfocused, lost in the memory. "David didn't shout. He didn't posture. He just... changed. One second, he was my son's eccentric father in law, rescuing a damsel in distress, the next... he was something else. Something silent and final. He moved so fast. He killed all three of them with that short sword he carries. It wasn't a fight, Callie. It was an extermination. It was over in less than thirty seconds."

She finally looked back at Callie, her eyes boring into her. "He has that same look in his eye right now. That quiet, focused calm. It's the scariest thing I've ever seen. The thing is, he found out later that my flat tire wasn't random. It was a trap, set for him by a man who helped him build this place. A man named Boyd."

Callie felt dizzy. "Boyd was a threat?" Lynn nodded slowly. "Boyd wasn't working alone either. He had help. Inside." She paused, letting the weight of her words land. "A nineteen-year-old girl named Kris. She was... close to David. I think she might have even loved him, in her own twisted way. But she was feeding information to Boyd." "So. what happened to her?" Callie asked, already dreading the answer. "David doesn't leave loose ends," Lynn said, her voice flat and devoid of emotion. "He doesn't leave witnesses or survivors who might come back for revenge. He didn't leave anyone alive from that group. Not Boyd. Not his men. Not even Kris."

"He... he killed her?" Callie's voice cracked. "A girl?" Lynn gave a single, sharp nod. "Yes. I was there. I watched the whole thing happen." Callie physically recoiled. She tried to picture it, tried to reconcile the image of David with that of a cold-blooded killer. The two images wouldn't merge. They were like oil and water in her mind. "Tell me," Callie said, her voice barely audible. It wasn't a request; it was a plea. She needed to understand the chasm that had just opened up at her feet.

Lynn took a slow breath, her eyes going distant as she looked back to that day a year ago. "We were at my parents' house. After David and his team cleared it, we were talking with my folks." She paused, painting the scene not just with words, but with the chilling atmosphere she recalled. "It was so... normal. Deceptively so. My mom made coffee. The house smelled like it always did, pot roast and Folgers. Kris was sitting on the couch, sipping from a mug like she belonged there. Like she was family. Josh and Lily were on the loveseat opposite her. Just a quiet conversation in the middle of the night."

Callie held her breath, her own crush on Junior feeling childish and frivolous in the face of this story. This was a world of different stakes. "David was talking to Boyd," Lynn continued, her voice low and even. "He was calm. He asked Boyd if he'd mind stepping into my brother's old room to discuss a partnership. Boyd, arrogant and unsuspecting, just followed him in."

Lynn stared at her hands. "David closed the door. Josh and Lily didn't even look up. Kris took another sip of coffee. I counted. I don't know why, but I counted. One... two... three... four... five. At five seconds, the door opened, and David walked out alone. He brushed his hands together. There wasn't a sound. No fight, no scream. Nothing. Later, I was in there gathering my parents stuff, and he was just laying on the bed. His larynx had been crushed."

Callie felt a wave of nausea. The heat of the night was suddenly oppressive. "And... Kris?" "When David walked back into the living room. He didn't raise his voice. He just looked at her, right over the rim of her coffee cup, and confronted her. Kris... she just shattered. The cup fell from her hands, shattering on the hardwood floor. Coffee went everywhere. First, she tried to deny it, rambling nonsense. But David's eyes... they don't allow for lies. He just watched her. Then she started sobbing, ugly, heaving sobs. She scrambled and ran to him."

Callie could see it, a desperate, broken girl running to the man she had betrayed, the man she probably loved in her own destructive way. "She threw her arms around his waist," Lynn's voice was almost a monotone now, stripped of all emotion. "She was begging. 'I'm sorry, I'm so sorry, please, I love you, please forgive me.' She buried her face in his chest."

A horrible, tiny sliver of hope pricked at Callie's imagination. Maybe he'd showed mercy. Maybe this was a cautionary tale, not an execution. "And David..." Lynn's eyes met Callie's, dark and haunted. "He embraced her. He wrapped his arms around her, holding the back of her head with one hand, almost like a father comforting a child. For a second, I thought he was going to forgive her. I saw his jaw clench, a flicker of something in his eyes, pity, maybe. He understood her weakness, her fear."

Lynn looked away, toward the darkness beyond the ranch's perimeter. "Then we heard it." "Heard what?" Callie whispered, dreading the answer. "A sound I'll never forget. It wasn't loud. It was... intimate. A series of sharp, dense cracks. Like snapping a bundle of dry twigs in your hands. Crack. Crack-crack. Her back, her ribs. He was so strong, and she was so small."

The air left Callie's lungs in a silent whoosh. Her bubbly personality, her entire worldview, was being systematically dismantled by this story. "Her sobbing stopped instantly. She just... went limp in his arms. He held her for another moment, then gently lowered her to the floor. There was no blood. No final scream. He'd broken her spine, collapsed her chest. It was as clean and as silent as what he did to Boyd. Then he walked outside to start loading my parents' things into the truck."

Silence stretched between them. Callie's mind was now just a loop of a single, horrifying concept. He hugged her to death. Her brain, in a desperate attempt to process the horror, latched onto the most bizarre detail. "So... no mess?" she blurted out, then a hand flew to her mouth, her eyes wide with self-recrimination. "Oh my God, I can't believe I just said that. I am so sorry, that was... wow. Wrong."

To her utter astonishment, the corners of Lynn's mouth twitched, then pulled into a small, weary smile. "Don't be. It's a valid, if startling, observation. And no. No mess. That's the point. It was... efficient." Lynn leaned forward. "You have to understand, Callie. I think a part of David, the part that loved her, the part that remembers what it's like to be a normal man, wanted to forgive her. He looked at her, and you could see the war going on behind his eyes. He wanted to let it go." "But he didn't," Callie said, her voice small.

"No. Because his mind wouldn't allow it," Lynn explained, tapping her own temple. "It's more than just him being smart or having lived through this before. It's like... his entire being, his soul, his conscience, has been broken and mended so many times that there's no flexibility left. Think of a bone that's been shattered and healed. It's stronger in that spot, but it's all scar tissue. It can't bend. If you put the wrong pressure on it, it won't give; it'll just snap again."

Her gaze was now filled with a sadness so profound it seemed to predate her own existence. "And I know about that scar tissue," she added, her voice dropping even lower, "because I'm responsible for some of the worst fractures," she said, her voice flat with the weight of the confession.

Callie's brain stuttered. She blinked, certain she'd misheard. "What? How? I don't understand." Lynn's weary smile returned, but this time it was laced with an unbearable sadness. "In the life before this one... the one only David remembers... I was his wife. We were married for nearly eighteen years." The statement landed in the quiet room with a thud. Callie's mouth opened, a string of confused protests forming in her mind.

"We had three sons," Lynn continued, her voice becoming distant, as if she were reciting a story she'd learned but never lived. "And I broke his heart. Then I broke his trust. We divorced about ten years before the world fell apart the first time. The official reason was irreconcilable differences. The real reason... was me. I could never fully trust him. He was always... different. Seeing things other people didn't, preparing us for... whatever. I probably just thought he was weird. I couldn't accept his form of love. My lack of faith in him eventually wore him down, chiseled away at him until we just... broke."

Callie was speechless, her mind reeling. This was a layer of history, of tragedy, she never could have imagined. She was talking to a ghost from David's past, a woman who carried the weight of a life she couldn't even recall. "That fracture... the divorce... that was bad," Lynn said, her voice dropping even lower, becoming raw. "But it wasn't the snap that shattered the bone. That came later." She paused, swallowing hard. "After the world ended the first time, our boys... they were like him. They inherited his mind, his intelligence. They were capable. But I... I still couldn't trust them. I couldn't trust their judgment because it was his judgment. I questioned them, held them back, made them doubt themselves at moments when hesitation was fatal."

A single tear traced a path down Lynn's cheek, shimmering in the lamplight. "And because of me... they all died. My sons. David's sons. My inability to trust the very man who was trying to take care of us." The air in the room grew heavy, charged with the phantom grief of three boys who, in this reality, had never existed. Callie felt a wave of nausea. This was too much. Too big. "But... how?" Callie finally managed, her voice cracking. "How can you know all of that? If you don't remember it?"

Lynn wiped her tear away with the back of her hand, a gesture of finality. A strange clarity settled in her eyes. "I don't. Not like a memory. I have no images, no sounds, no feelings from that life. When I first met David because of Josh, I didn't trust him this time either. Then David rescued me this time around, eventually, he told me. He laid it all out. And the moment he said it... I knew."

Chapter 27:

Edged Weapons Only

David, the architect of this departure, moved through the farewells with an economy of motion and emotion. Dressed in tactical gear, his wakizashi a line of tradition against his hip and a Beretta a familiar pressure on his thigh, he was the calm eye of the storm. Tiffany adjusted the collar of his vest, a silent question in her touch. "You have everything?" "Everything but a guarantee, my love," he answered, his lips brushing her forehead, his smile smoothing the worry from her face. "But we're the next best thing."

Jennifer, a playful glint in her eyes, ran a hand down his armored chest. "Bring them hell, Master," she purred. He cupped her cheek for a brief moment. "Only if they're foolish enough to open the door for it." From the porch, Jessica's voice, laced with its signature sarcasm, cut through the tension. "Don't go getting yourself killed, Daddy. The girls and I have a betting pool on how many you'll take down, and I put a lot of good chocolate on 'all of them.'"

His gaze then found Nicole. She stood apart, her hands clutched, her face a mask of taut anxiety. Their daughter, Grace, was the reason for the armor and the engines. David crossed to her, his expression softening. He offered no hollow comforts, only the solid grip of his hand in hers. "We're going to get the people who did this," he said, his voice low and certain. "We'll find their tracks. We'll finish this." A single tear traced a path through the dust on her cheek. "Bring our son home too," she whispered.

That son, Seth, was experiencing his own farewell under the shade of a sprawling oak. Looking more man than boy in his gear, he held the hands of Bonnie, whose father stood a respectful distance away. Bonnie's eyes shone as she pulled Seth's head down, her kiss a desperate, passionate promise of forever, a silent plea for his return.

Nearby, Junior endured a goodbye of a different flavor. His wives, Emma, Olivia, and Riley, moved with efficiency, checking magazines, handing over a canteen, a quick, hard kiss. Then Callie burst through the crowd, a whirlwind of frantic energy, throwing her arms around his neck. "You come back to me, you hear?!" she demanded into his shoulder. "If a bullet even thinks about coming near you, you tell it that Callie said 'no'!"

Junior, his voice a flat monotone of patience, gently pried her loose. "I'll be careful, Callie." Her dramatic facade cracked, revealing the genuine fear beneath. "Just... come home, we need you." He offered her a rare, small smile. "Always do." Turning to his team, his voice became steel. "Alright folks, saddle up!"

David took one last look at the family assembled on the porch. Elena watched him from inside The Beast, fascinated by the infinitesimal shifts in his expression as he processed a dozen variables at once. "Alright," he said into his comms. "Let's go hunting."

The Beast snarled and spat gravel. The heavy Transit rumbled in its wake, and the sedan fell in behind. The convoy coiled out of the compound and onto the dusty track, heading east toward the rising sun and an unseen enemy. On the porch, the women watched until the dust swallowed the last vehicle, leaving only the heat, the humming quiet, and their shared, unshakeable faith.

Inside the rattling confines of the armored van, the men who had left the porch were gone. Emma, strapped into her seat, fixed her gaze on the back of her husband's head. The man who held her with gentle strength, who offered that heart-stopping smile, had been replaced. In his place was the final boss fight of a vengeful sibling, the man who had rescued her. His posture was ramrod straight, his eyes constantly scanning from the road to the mirrors, an efficiency that was both awe-inspiring and chilling.

Beside him, Seth was a mirror image of that same focus. The kind, fifteen-year-old boy who did chores and kissed his love goodbye had vanished. This was a different Seth, his young face a hard mask, his hands resting on his rifle with an unsettling familiarity. "You're staring," Riley murmured from beside Emma, her voice low but edged with its usual sarcasm. "It's his murder face. You get used to it. Mostly. Kinda hot, in a 'please don't disembowel me for leaving my socks on the floor' sort of way."

Emma managed a weak smile, grateful for the levity. "It's… scary." "That's the point, sweetcheeks," Riley said, her expression softening. "Look at the boys."

Emma's gaze shifted. Across the aisle, Caleb checked his gear for the fifth time, his movements laced with a frantic energy. Andrew rhythmically tapped his fingers against his thigh armor, a silent drumbeat of anxiety. Marvin stared straight ahead, a muscle twitching in his jaw. They were proficient, their gear stowed, their weapons ready. But they were young soldiers, wire-taut with an equal measure of eagerness and fear.

Then her eyes found Parker, sitting near the back. The former army scout was the picture of tranquility. He wasn't tense; he was coiled. His eyes were half-lidded, but they missed nothing. He had a calm, almost placid expression, the look of a man who had not only been here and done that, but had also bought the t-shirt, lost it, and didn't feel the need to buy another. The others had the focused expressions of men heading into a fight. Parker had the tired, seasoned expression of a man for whom the fight had never really ended. The new recruits, for all their training under Junior, lacked that profound weariness. This was an event for them. For Parker, Emma suspected, it was just Sunday.

Up front, at the wheel, David was an island of calm in a sea of his own making. To a stranger, his relaxed posture and contemplative expression might suggest a man lost in mundane thought, perhaps pondering the day's trivialities. But Elena, sitting behind him, knew better. She had made a study of the man she loved, and she could read the storm raging beneath the placid surface. It was in the subtle tension of his shoulders, a rigid line beneath his dark shirt.

It was in the cold, analytical fire of his eyes as they dissected the terrain. His fury wasn't loud; it was a contained, thermonuclear core, meticulously compartmentalized and aimed. She knew precisely where its most potent totem lay: in his right pocket, a deformed piece of metal, a small, heavy lump that was once a bullet. The bullet that had torn through their friend Kyle and nearly claimed Grace.

"Dirt track on the right, about a quarter-mile up," Scott's voice was a low rasp from the passenger seat. His thick finger pointed, a stark contrast to David's quiet control. "That'll lead us to the trap site, and closer to the perimeter of the first settlement. The one Josh's drone tagged as 'Patriot's Rest'."

A flicker of dry humor, sharp as flint, touched David's voice. "Patriot's Rest. Sounds delightful. I hope they don't have tacky lawn gnomes." Elena leaned forward, her voice a low purr meant only for him. "Is it getting warm in here, or is that just your rage threatening to set the upholstery on fire?" A ghost of a smile touched David's lips. "A little of both, my love," he replied, his gaze meeting hers in the rearview mirror. Beside Elena, Noah sat as a silent specter, his enormous .338 MRAD rifle propped vertically beside him.

In the last vehicle, a comfortable sedan, the atmosphere was markedly different. Darrel drove with a practiced ease, one hand on the wheel. Beside him, Reagan fidgeted, a nervous energy radiating from her. In the back, Josh was hunched over a tablet, running pre-flight checks on a dormant drone, while Lily sat next to him, her rifle across her lap.

The comfortable quiet was broken by Reagan. "Hey, can I ask a weird question?" Darrel glanced at her, an eyebrow raised in amusement. "Reagan, in this family, 'weird' is the baseline. Shoot." "It's about Grace," Reagan said, her voice dropping slightly. "Andrea said the bullet that hit her didn't break a single bone, even from under 150 yards. How is that possible? A round with that much force should have shattered something."

The question hung in the air-conditioned space. Lily, who had been watching the road, shook her head. "I don't know. Luck, maybe? A miracle?" Darrel chuckled. He caught Lily's eye in the mirror. "Alright, follow-up question. Has anyone in David's direct bloodline, and I mean you, Seth, Grace, Junior, ever actually broken a bone?"

Lily blinked, the question catching her off guard. She mentally scrolled back through twenty-one years of a life that was anything but gentle, climbing, training, fighting, the chaotic reality of being David's daughter. The scrapes, the bruises, the cuts were countless. But a break? A snap? The jarring finality of fractured bone? The memory wasn't there. "Huh," she said slowly, a strange realization dawning. "You know… I don't think so. Not once." She looked at Josh. "You ever known Junior to break anything?" Josh shook his head without looking up from his tablet. "Nope. Never."

A voice crackled over the radio. It was David. "Convoy, halt. We're at the site. Maintain alert status." Lily, still buzzing, climbed out of the sedan, Josh close behind her. He was already unfolding the drone from its travel case, his brow furrowed with concentration. Darrel and Reagan followed, Darrel stretching theatrically, popping his back with a loud crack.

Ahead, David stood beside 'The Beast,' surveying the scene with Elena at his side. Noah and Scott, grim-faced,

45

flanked them, weapons at the ready. Behind them, Junior efficiently directed the passengers from the Ford Transit, Emma and Riley flanking him. "Josh, get that bird in the air," David commanded "Let's get a quick peek at what we're walking into." Josh nodded, his fingers flying over the drone's controls. The small quadcopter whirred to life, rising swiftly into the air.

The large 18-foot net corral sat abandoned in the clearing, a trail of dried blood near the road. "This is where it happened," Scott said, looking at the trap. Lily scanned the perimeter, then moved towards the trap, her eyes scanning the ground. "Footprints," she announced, her voice sharp and clear. Josh, distracted by the drone feed, paused, his attention snapping back to Lily. "Heavy ones. All over the baited area."

She crouched, examining the prints more closely. "They came back. For the rest of the pigs." Darrel sauntered over, peering at the footprints. "Well, duh. You don't just leave a buffet sitting out in the open, do you? Especially when you're probably living on squirrels and dandelion greens."

David, who had been listening intently, approached. He surveyed the scene, his expression unreadable. "Josh, what are you seeing on the drone feed?" Josh tapped at the screen, zooming in on the surrounding woods. "Nothing obvious, David. Just trees, brush, and... wait. There's movement. About a hundred yards east, in those trees. Looks like... people." "How many?" David asked, his voice tightening. "Hard to tell exactly," Josh replied, squinting at the screen. "At least five, maybe more."

A beat of silence passed. David needed no more. "Josh, kill the drone. Power it down completely. We're going in quiet." He turned to the assembled group, his eyes sweeping over them. "Team formations. Lily, you take Team Three and hold our back-right flank. Junior, Team Two, you have our middle-left. My team is on point. We move in now."

He paused. "Weapons discipline. Edged only for the initial contact. Everyone else, provide cover. A single gunshot from them or us means we go loud. Understood?" A series of muted clicks and soft rustles was the only reply as rifles were slung and pistols were holstered. The practiced efficiency was terrifying in its normalcy. Darrel grinned, giving his kamas a theatrical flourish. "My girls have been itching for a dance."

Emma stared. A cold knot of dread formed in her stomach. She watched as Lily drew her short blades, her expression as placid as if she were about to peel potatoes. She saw David unsheathe the wicked curve of his wakizashi. These were people she ate dinner with, people who joked and laughed. Now, they were preparing for silent, intimate killing.

Is he serious? she thought, her gaze snapping to her husband. Edged weapons? Her shock curdled into outright disbelief when she saw what Junior was pulling from its sheath on his hip. It wasn't a knife. It was a tomahawk, its polished steel head gleaming ominously in the dappled sunlight. Emma felt a hand on her arm and jumped. It was Riley, her face a mask of sarcastic nonchalance. "Don't worry, sweetie." she murmured. "They're good with their hands."

Emma couldn't process the comment. She stumbled closer to Junior, her voice a frantic whisper that was barely audible. "A tomahawk, Junior? Seriously?" Junior didn't answer with words. He simply turned and cupped her face in his free hand. He leaned in and kissed her, a firm, possessive press of lips that was both a reassurance and a promise. It sent a disorienting jolt through her, a dizzying mix of fear, love, and a strange, thrilling excitement. The kiss ended, but the feeling lingered, a funny, fluttering sensation in her chest. She was about to see the man she loved do what she had only imagined up till now.

She watched him move ahead with Team 2, the tomahawk held loosely at his side. He moved with an unnerving grace, his steps as silent as the rest of them. To her right, David led Team 1, his expression as placid as a calm lake. He held the wakizashi with a swordsman's familiarity. Behind him, Scott carried his rifle at a low ready, while young Seth crept along, his gaze sharp and observant, his hands empty but close to the knives on his belt. Team 3, with Lily at the point, mirrored the movements of the left flank. Lily's short blades were reverse-gripped in her hands, her posture relaxed but coiled, like a panther ready to spring. Darrel was a shadow behind her, the sickles of his kamas looking utterly alien in the Texas woods.

David raised a closed fist. The entire war party, all fifteen of them, froze in unison. The silence was absolute, broken only by the incessant buzz of insects and the distant coo of a morning dove. Emma held her breath, her heart hammering against her ribs. Up ahead, through a thicket of yaupon holly, was a small clearing. A smoldering campfire sent a thin ribbon of smoke into the humid air. Five men were scattered around it, looking rumpled and lazy. Rifles, mostly AK variants, were propped against logs or packs, carelessly close but not in their hands. They were talking in low mumbles, one of them scratching at a bug bite on his neck.

David gave a slow, deliberate hand signal. Forward. Edged only. Hold fire unless engaged. Emma's stomach twisted. He's really doing it. David, Seth, and Elena broke from cover, moving into the clearing with no more sound than a gentle breeze. On the opposite side, Lily and Darrel did the same. And from the center, Junior advanced, his tomahawk no longer at his side but held in a ready grip. The overwatch teams—Scott, Parker, Josh, and the others fanned out, finding cover and aiming their rifles, their safeties clicking off with barely a whisper.

One of the men by the fire looked up, bleary-eyed, and saw David first. His eyes went from David's face to the gleaming wakizashi. A slow, disbelieving grin spread across his face. He nudged the man next to him. "Hey. Hey, Earl. Get a load of this," he snorted, not even bothering to lower his voice.

Earl looked, then another, and soon all five of them were staring. The initial confusion melted into open, derisive laughter. "What in the hell?" one chuckled, pointing a greasy finger at Junior. "You bring a hatchet to a gunfight, boy?" Another howled, slapping his knee as he eyed Lily's blades. "Look at the little lady! Think she's gonna gut a fish with them things?"

49

A third, a burly man with a tangled beard who seemed to be their leader, leaned back against his pack, a smug look on his face. "Well, now. Looks like the Renaissance Faire came to town early this year. What's next? You gonna challenge us to a duel for our honor?"

The men erupted in cackles, their mockery echoing through the quiet woods. They made no move for their weapons. Why would they? Before them stood a handful of people armed with what looked like museum pieces and farming tools. They were threats in the same way a theatrical troupe was a threat.

From her position, Emma saw David's eyes flick to the side of the laughing leader. Propped against a log, within arm's reach, was a dull black AK-47 with a banana clip. No words were exchanged. No new signal was given. The plan was already in motion. The laughter died in a wet choke.

David had closed the ten feet between them in two silent strides. The wakizashi came up in a blur, the motion fluid and obscenely fast. The razor-sharp edge met the leader's jaw and didn't stop, severing his head from the mouth up. Before the man's laughing cronies could even process the fountain of blood that erupted from their leader's open head, David pivoted. With the full force of his strength, he brought the sword down in a diagonal arc, striking the man at the collarbone. There was a sickening, wet crunch as the blade sheared through flesh, bone, and organs, exiting cleanly at the opposite hip. The man's body, now in two diagonally-bisected, twitching halves, collapsed into a heap on the ground.

Simultaneously, the man who had mocked Lily found her suddenly in his personal space. His eyes widened in shock, his mouth opening to scream. He never got the chance. Lily's right hand darted out, her blade sinking deep into his throat. With a flick of her wrist, she opened his carotid artery as she spun past him. Her left hand came around in the same fluid motion, the second blade plunging hilt-deep under the ribs of the man next to him, straight into his heart. Both men crumpled to the ground, one gurgling, the other already dead. It had taken less than two seconds.

The fourth man, the one who'd called Junior's tomahawk a hatchet, finally reacted, scrambling desperately for his SKS. He was too slow. Junior was on him, the tomahawk swinging in a deceptively simple, brutal arc. The sharpened beard of the axe head caught the man square in the face, hooking into his cheekbone and nose with a sound like a melon splitting open. Junior didn't pull it out. He simply put his weight into it, wrenching downward. The man's face tore open. As he fell backwards, screaming through a ruined visage, Junior reversed his grip and swung the tomahawk again, the spike on the back of the head burying itself deep in the man's groin.

The last man, his face a mask of pure, abject terror, had managed to lunge for his rifle. His fingers were just brushing the stock when a flash of steel crossed the clearing. A hard THWACK echoed as Seth's throwing knife, hurled with impossible precision, pinned the man's hand to the trunk of the pine tree he was leaning against. A piercing shriek of agony finally broke the combat silence, the man staring in horror at the blade that had stapled him to the wood.

Emma felt as if her lungs had forgotten how to draw air. The scene was almost deafening. Four bodies lay twisted on the forest floor, dispatched with a terrifying swiftness by a handful of people she shared breakfast with. The knot in her stomach, which had been a cold stone of dread just minutes before, had morphed into something else entirely. It was a dizzying, electric thrill that sang along her nerves, a primal hum of attraction and terror.

She looked at Junior, her husband, leaning casually on his blood-soaked tomahawk. He had just torn a man's face off and then impaled him with the same weapon, and now he looked as placid as if he were waiting for a pot of coffee to brew. This was the unleashed fury he wielded at David's command, a force of nature she had willingly bound herself to. It was horrifying. It was intoxicating.

David broke the stillness. With the serene focus of a surgeon cleaning his instruments, he wiped the crimson from his wakizashi onto the dead leader's shirt, the fabric absorbing the stain. He sheathed the short sword with a soft, decisive click. He walked towards the last survivor, his footsteps unnervingly quiet on the bed of pine needles. The man, whose shrieks had subsided into choked, hysterical sobs, watched him approach, his eyes wide with terror.

David stopped directly in front of him. He reached into his pocket and produced a small, metallic object. He held it between his thumb and forefinger, letting the morning sun glint off the deformed copper jacket of the bullet. He held it up close to the man's face. His voice, when he spoke, was calm, almost professorial. "This bullet," he began, his tone soft, a stark contrast to the violence surrounding them, "nearly killed my daughter." He paused, letting the words hang in the heavy air. "We tracked the shooter here. To this camp."

The pinned man shook his head violently, snot and tears flying from his face. "No! It wasn't me! I swear to God, it wasn't me! I wasn't even out yesterday! I was here! I didn't do it!" he babbled, his voice cracking with desperation. David simply looked at him, his expression unreadable.

From beside a nearby oak, Junior shifted his weight. He let out a theatrical sigh and shrugged, the gesture so casual it was utterly jarring. "Well, that settles that, I guess," he said, his voice laced with a strange sort of finality. "Guess we have to let him go." The pinned man's sobbing hitched, replaced by a stunned, hopeful silence. He looked from Junior's impassive face to David's. In the tree line, Caleb lowered his rifle slightly, exchanging a bewildered look with Reagan.

David nodded slowly, a thoughtful expression on his face. "Of course," he agreed, his voice still gentle. "He says he didn't do it. Then he didn't do it." This was too much for Darrel. He cautiously broke cover, his pair of kamas hanging from his hands, and approached the inner circle of carnage. "Hold on," he said. "Are y'all serious? We're just gonna… let him go?"

Junior turned his head to look at Darrel, his eyes flat. He gestured with his chin towards the man stapled to the tree. "Well, we can't just leave him there, Darrel. That's just rude."

He then pointed the handle of his tomahawk towards Seth, who was quietly standing by. "Besides, Seth needs his knife back. That's a good knife."

Junior took a step closer to the prisoner, lowering his voice into a conspiratorial tone that carried clearly in the quiet clearing. He gave a slight nod, as if sharing a profound truth. "Plus," he added, his face completely deadpan. "He said he didn't do it." A beat of absolute silence followed, in which the sheer, dark absurdity of the statement settled over the new recruits. Emma saw Lily suppress a grim smile. Parker simply shook his head slowly.

The prisoner's face, tear-streaked and dirty, was a mask of dawning, idiotic relief. "Yeah! Yeah, I didn't!" he blubbered, nodding vigorously. "I didn't do it! You can let me go, I swear, I won't tell anyone." "Okay, okay, calm down," Junior said, holding up a placating hand. He stepped right up to the man, his movements smooth and economical. "We'll get you out of there. Just hold still." He rested one hand on the man's pinned shoulder, as if to steady him. With his other hand, he raised his tomahawk. The prisoner flinched, but Junior's voice was a soothing baritone. "Easy now."

Then, in one fluid, brutal motion, Junior swung the tomahawk. It wasn't a hacking chop, but a precise, powerful cut. There was a single, meaty thump followed by the wet snap of bone. The blade sheared clean through the man's upper arm, just above the elbow, severing the limb in a spray of arterial red that painted the oak's bark.

The man didn't even have time to register what had happened before the agony hit him. A raw, piercing shriek tore from his throat, a sound of pure, animal terror that sent a flock of birds scattering from the canopy above. He stared in disbelief at the stump of his arm, which was now gushing blood, then at his own severed limb, still grotesquely pinned to the tree by Seth's knife.

Without a word, Seth stepped forward, his expression unchanged. He gripped the severed forearm, worked his knife free from the hand and the tree trunk, and wiped the blade meticulously on the sleeve still wrapped around the arm. He slid the clean knife back into its sheath on his belt and stepped back, his part in the macabre play concluded.

The one-armed man, now free, stumbled back from the tree. His mind had clearly snapped, running on nothing but primal fear. He clutched his gushing stump with his remaining hand and, with a choked, panicked sob, he turned and ran. He crashed through the underbrush, a frantic, screaming mess, heading southeast.

No one moved to stop him. Junior simply stood there, watching him go, his tomahawk resting casually on his shoulder. He let the man cover twenty, then forty yards, his screams growing fainter. The other teams watched in a stunned, silent tableau, the scene unfolding like a fever dream.

Then, with the same casual air he'd used to sigh, Junior shifted his stance. He brought the tomahawk up, his arm a blur of practiced motion. The weapon spun end over end, a perfect, silent spiral of polished wood and sharpened steel, arcing through the humid air. It tracked the running man's path with unerring accuracy.

The tomahawk covered the distance in a little over a second. It buried itself in the back of the man's skull with a sickening thunk that was audible even from their position. The man's legs went out from under him, and he pitched forward into a thicket of ferns, instantly silent and still. The clearing was quiet again, save for the buzzing of insects.

After a long moment, a sound broke the tension. It was a low chuckle. Everyone turned to look at Darrel. A slow grin was spreading across his face, the initial shock replaced by dawning comprehension and a dark appreciation for the violent theater he'd just witnessed.

He shook his head, the kamas in his hands seeming less like weapons and more like props. "Okay," he breathed, the laugh still in his voice. "Okay, I get it now." He gestured with his head in the direction the man had run. "At least now we know which way their camp is." David clapped a hand on Darrel's shoulder, a faint, proud smile on his own lips. "Exactly," he said, his voice warm with approval. "Southeast. Now, let's go get Junior's tomahawk back. That's a good tomahawk."

Chapter 28:

The Fork and the Road

David, having retrieved Junior's tomahawk from the scout's skull, gave it a cursory wipe on the man's trousers. "Good steel," he commented absently, the words barely audible amidst the rustling leaves. He cocked his arm back, the motion deceptively casual, and launched the tomahawk. It wasn't a throw. It was a delivery system. The tomahawk spun end-over-end with terrifying precision, a blur of motion that resembled a small, darkly gleaming helicopter blade. The distance between David and Junior evaporated in a heartbeat.

Emma, eyes wide and fixed on Junior's back, gasped. Her hand flew to her mouth, stifling a scream. The sheer audacity of the throw, the implied threat contained within its arc, was breathtaking. She had seen Junior in action many times, but even she was still susceptible to the man's raw power. Junior, however, didn't even flinch. He caught the tomahawk by the haft, the spinning blade coming to a dead stop inches from his fingers. He didn't even glance at it.

Riley, practically vibrating with excitement, latched onto Emma's arm. "That's our husband!" she squealed, her voice a giddy whisper. "Isn't he amazing?" She beamed at Emma, completely oblivious to the initial shock that had registered on the other woman's face. Caleb, who had been diligently practicing knife-catching with Darrel, winced sympathetically for Emma. He knew firsthand how jarring

Junior's casual displays of lethality could be. "Yeah, well, try catching that when it's aimed at you," he muttered under his breath, earning him a playful jab from Andrew.

With a series of hand signals so subtle they were nearly imperceptible, he set the three teams into motion. They moved through the overgrown Texas scrubland with the practiced efficiency of a wolf pack on the hunt. They skirted the edge of a withered cornfield, using the tall, dead stalks as cover, until they reached a small rise overlooking their target. Below them lay a plot of land, dominated by a large, single-story farmhouse that had seen better days. A dilapidated barn stood off to one side, its red paint peeling like sunburnt skin. A few hastily constructed wooden outposts, little more than glorified deer stands, guarded the perimeter.

"Down," David whispered, and fifteen people melted into the terrain. Scott was already prone, his binoculars fixed on the settlement. Parker, his contemporary, watched from the left flank. The rest of the teams found their own positions, weapons oriented towards the potential threat, forming a crescent of lethal overwatch. "What do you see, Scotty?" David asked. Scott didn't look away from his lenses. "God damn it David, I thought I told you to stop calling me that. Got four tangos visible. Two on the front porch, one by the barn, one in the east outpost. All male. All armed." He paused, adjusting the focus knob. "And there's our first problem, boss."

"Talk to me," David prompted. "The hardware," Scott clarified. "I'm looking at AR-15s. Standard 5.56 platforms. One guy on the porch has what looks like a Glock on his hip. I don't see a single SKS or AK variant. Not a lick of 7.62x39 out there." A ripple of uncertainty passed through the group. Their primary lead, the bullet that had torn through Kyle and shattered Grace's body, pointed to a specific type of weapon. These weren't it.

David processed the new data. The settlement was heavily armed. And they were camped less than a mile from where his family had been attacked. Coincidence was a luxury he didn't believe in. He motioned for Junior and Lily to crawl over to his position. "Report," he commanded. "Weapons don't match," Lily stated, her brow furrowed in concentration. "Could be a different group entirely." "Or," Junior countered, his voice a low growl, "this is just the welcoming committee. The guys with the Kalashnikovs could be inside, waiting. It's not unheard of to arm your outer sentries with more common ammo."

"Both are possibilities," David conceded. He looked back towards the farmhouse, his eyes narrowed. "We can't confirm they're our shooters based on what we see. That changes things. But that doesn't mean they're friendly, so how about we go ask?" He looked from Junior to Lily, and then his gaze settled on Seth, who had remained silent, watching the property. An idea coalesced, a plan that was equal parts deception and intelligence gathering. "We go in soft," David announced. "A diplomatic approach."

Junior looked at his father as if he'd just suggested they take up knitting. "Diplomatic? Dad, these aren't people you negotiate with." "I'm not negotiating, son. I'm gathering information," David corrected him patiently. "They won't

59

give it to us if we start stacking bodies at their doorstep. We need to know who they are, how many there are, and what they have inside that house before we commit." He turned to Seth. "Seth, you're with me."

Seth blinked. "Me, dad?" David simply nodded. "Father and son on a hiking trip, how's that sound?" Without saying a word, Seth unslung his rifle and handed it to Noah, whose quiet gaze followed them. Noah gave Seth a subtle, almost imperceptible nod. It was an agreement solidified in silence, a promise made between two young men.

David and Seth backed away from their concealed position, leaving the formidable firepower of their family coiled like a snake in the tall grass. They circled around, emerging onto the dusty, cracked asphalt of the old county road as if they'd been walking it all morning. The sun was climbing, its heat already baking the air and shimmering off the pavement.

"So," David said, his voice light and conversational, a stark contrast to the grim tension of the last hour. He fell into an easy, ambling gait. "What was Noah's agreement?" Seth glanced at his father, his young face a mask of teenage stoicism. He was used to his father's uncanny ability to perceive everything, but it was still embarrassing. He stuffed his hands in his pockets, kicking at a loose stone. "It's nothing," he mumbled.

"It was significant enough for him to give you the 'I'm counting on you, buddy' look," David pressed gently. "I'm not interrogating you, son. I'm curious. In my experience, pacts made by fifteen-year-old boys in the middle of a potential firefight tend to be… interesting." Seth sighed, the sound heavy with the burden of his friend's request. He looked away towards the farmhouse, now visible through a break in the trees. "He wants us to save the Latinas."

David stopped walking. He turned to face his son, a slow, deeply amused smile spreading across his face. He processed the statement with the same analytical intensity he'd applied to the settlement's defenses. "Plural," he noted. "As in, all of them?" "I don't know, he just wants one for himself," Seth said. "Did he have specific ones picked out?" David continued, his tone now one of genuine academic inquiry. "Is there a catalog we should be aware of? Are we operating on a 'you'll know them when you see them' basis? Because frankly, son, our operational intelligence on the romantic proclivities of the local hostile populace is severely lacking."

"I mean, it's not a big deal," Seth stammered, his gaze fixed firmly on a dilapidated fence post in the distance. "It's just… guy stuff." David chuckled, a low, rumbling sound. "I was a 'guy' once, son. And 'guy stuff' right before storming a compound that shot your sister tends to involve either profound last words or profoundly stupid requests. Given Noah's general stoicism, I'm betting on the latter. So, why the plural? Did he provide a list of desired attributes? A type? We need actionable intelligence here."

Seth let out an exasperated breath, finally giving in. "He just has a thing for them, okay? Always has." "A noble aspiration," David mused, his eyes scanning the crude fortifications of the farmhouse ahead. "But why didn't he just make a move on Sophia when they were all rescued? She's a lovely girl. Smart, capable. Definitely meets the general criteria of being a latina." Seth kicked at a clump of dry grass. "He said... and don't look at me like that... he said she's too 'Caucasian' for him."

David paused mid-stride, his head tilting slightly. He brought a hand to his chin, stroking his stubble as if processing a complex tactical problem. "Fascinating. A specific aesthetic preference. That narrows the search considerably. It's an oddly specific filter to apply during the apocalypse. So, Sophia didn't meet the criteria?" "It wasn't just that," Seth added quickly. "Caleb liked her. Since Basic Training, apparently. Before any of us even knew who she was. So, when Junior brought them all back, the guys... they had a kind of gentlemen's agreement. Sophia was off-limits. She was Caleb's to win or lose."

David's eyebrows shot up in genuine surprise, and the amused smile returned, warmer this time. "A gentlemen's agreement," he repeated. He looked from his son back towards the settlement. "In a world where men kill each other over a can of beans and a handful of bullets, they established a code of romantic honor." He shook his head slowly, a look of profound, paternal pride on his face. "That's... honorable. Genuinely archaic and honorable. I approve."

He clapped a heavy, reassuring hand on Seth's shoulder. "Well, you can't let that kind of nobility go unrewarded. It's a foundational principle of a functioning society. You reward good behavior." He grinned, a flash of mischief in his eyes. "Objective Two, secondary but important for morale: We identify and secure a potential partner for Noah, provided she is a) Latina, and b) not interested in staying with her current… associates."

Seth stared at his father, dumbfounded. "You're serious?" "Completely," David said, his tone shifting back to business as they reached the edge of the overgrown lawn that marked the property line. "Consider me his wingman. A good sniper deserves a good spotter, and a good man deserves a shot at happiness. It's just… our methods of introduction will be a bit more aggressive than buying her a drink."

The overgrown lawn, once someone's pride, was now a knee-high sea of brown grass and opportunistic weeds. At its center stood the clapboard house. On the porch, two men in mismatched camo gear lounged in rickety chairs, their rifles held with a lazy familiarity that spoke more of boredom than discipline.

As David and Seth stepped from the tree line onto the edge of the dying lawn, both porch-sitters snapped to attention. The one on the left, a gaunt man with a patchy beard, raised his rifle. "That's far enough!" he barked, his voice raspy. David offered a placid smile, holding his hands up in a universally placating gesture. "Good morning," he called out, his voice carrying easily in the still morning air. "Lovely day for it. We were just in the area and thought we'd say hello."

The second guard, younger but with the same hollowed-out look, squinted at them. His eyes traveled from David's clean, well-maintained gear to Seth's healthy complexion. "You two look… well-fed," he said, the words laced with suspicion and a raw, gnawing envy. "Clean living and a positive attitude," David replied cheerfully. "We highly recommend it. It does wonders for the constitution." Seth remained silent, his hand resting near the throwing knives on his belt, his eyes flicking between the two men, the windows of the house, and the surrounding yard, cataloging every detail.

The first guard pushed himself off his chair and stomped down the porch steps, his rifle leveled at David's chest. "You ain't sayin' hello. You're snoopin'. And you ain't comin' any closer with that pig-sticker on your hip." He jabbed his rifle barrel towards David's wakizashi. "Leave it on the ground."

David let out a theatrical sigh. "If you insist. I wouldn't want to spoil the welcome." With practiced grace, he unbuckled the sheathed sword, held it horizontally for a moment, and then bent to place it gently in the grass. He did the same with his Beretta. "You, too, son," he said without looking at Seth. Seth reluctantly unstrapped his sheaths of throwing knives, placing them next to his father's weapons on the ground, feeling naked and exposed.

Just as they straightened up, the front door of the house creaked open. Two more men emerged, their movements more purposeful than the porch guards. They were armed with weathered but functional AK-platform rifles, the distinctive curved magazines a confirmation of Junior's Rule of Engagement. They were bigger, healthier-looking than the sentries, and they flanked the doorway with an air of authority. One of them, a burly man with a shaved head, jerked his chin towards the house. "Boss is gonna want to talk to you. Let's go." "Of course," David said, his smile never wavering. "Lead the way."

From his concealed position in a dense copse of oak trees fifty yards to the northwest, Noah watched the entire exchange through the powerful scope of his rifle. The crosshairs settled momentarily on the shaved head of the man who had ordered them inside. He saw David place his wakizashi in the grass. He saw Seth disarm. A cold, professional calm settled over him, but underneath it, a sliver of dark humor pricked at his mind. Step one: get captured. Bold strategy.

Riley leaned imperceptibly closer to Junior, whispering from the side of her mouth. "Well, there goes the element of surprise. I was hoping for a quieter party." On the right flank, hidden in a washout, Josh kept his M4 trained on the side of the house, his cheek welded to the stock. "Two more, AKs," he murmured to Lily beside him. "Four total outside. They're taking them in." Lily nodded, her eyes scanning the windows of the house.

As David and Seth were escorted up the creaking porch steps, David leaned slightly towards his son, his voice a low, instructional murmur. "Notice the hierarchy, Seth. The outside guards are thin, jumpy. Expendable. The inside guards are heavier, more confident. They get a larger share of the resources. Simple primate dominance behavior." Seth nodded, his gaze fixed forward. He was learning, always learning. His father wasn't just walking into a trap; he was dissecting it piece by piece as he went.

65

The interior of the house smelled of stale sweat, unwashed bodies, and despair. The door swung shut behind them with a heavy, final thud, plunging them into the dim light and cutting them off from the world outside. One of the guards shoved Seth forward slightly. David merely gave his son a reassuring look, a glint of serene confidence in his eyes that was utterly at odds with their surroundings. "And now," he whispered, his voice filled with an almost joyous anticipation, "for the pleasantries."

The large room they were herded into was the house's main living area, now a den of squalor and humanity. six sets of eyes, wary and hostile, settled on them. A large, bearded man sat on a makeshift throne, borne from an old recliner, a rusty AK-47 resting across his lap. He was the alpha, the center of this grim little universe. The air, thick with the smell of unwashed bodies and burnt cooking oil, felt heavy enough to choke on.

The man on the crate throne, whose name they would later learn was Hector, gestured with his chin. "Well, look what the cat dragged in. Two of 'em. Unarmed and lookin' lost. Where you from?" David's expression remained placid, a sea of calm in a room full of agitated currents. "We have a ranch," he said, his voice even and conversational. "About five miles to the west of here."

Hector's eyes narrowed, a flicker of recognition and anger in their depths. He leaned forward, the springs of his makeshift seat groaning in protest. "A ranch, huh? Funny. Lost a few of my boys out that way a while back. They went on a supply run and never came home. You wouldn't know anything about that, would you?" "I'm sorry for your loss," David said, the sincerity in his voice a stark contrast to the menace in Hector's. "The world is a dangerous place."

"It's about to get a lot more dangerous for you," Hector snarled, shifting the rifle on his lap. "I figure you owe me. Reparations. For my men. Whatever you got at that ranch of yours... it's mine now. A toll for passing through my territory and a price for my lost people." Seth stood perfectly still, his muscles coiled but his face a mask of neutrality. He watched his father, cataloging this exchange. This was a negotiation under duress, a chess match where the other player thought he'd already won.

David cocked his head slightly, a gesture of mild curiosity. "Before we discuss reparations," he said pleasantly, "I have a question for you. It looks like you've eaten well recently. Fresh meat, by the smell of it. Where did you get it?" One of the guards, the younger one, stammered, "W-we found 'em! Just lyin' there, all penned up. Figured someone wasn't comin' back for 'em." Hector's face contorted with rage. He slammed his fist on the table, making Seth flinch. "Damn it! Shut your trap!" He turned back to David, his eyes blazing. "So, what? You think those were your pigs? You think you can come in here, accuse us of stealing your damn dinner, and get away with it?"

A slow, compassionate smile spread across David's face, the kind a father gives a child who has just made a simple, correctable error. "Ah," he said, nodding. "Those pigs. My daughter trapped those. She's quite clever. She was setting them up so we could start a breeding program." He looked back at Hector, his smile unwavering. "So, you see, you haven't eaten on your own good fortune. You've eaten my food. Technically, you owe me for the provisions."

The room went silent, the tension broken by a sudden, booming laugh from Hector. It was a cruel, mocking sound that echoed off the grimy walls. The other men joined in, a chorus of jeers and sneers. "Your daughter?" Hector sputtered, wiping a tear of mirth from his eye. "You mean that little girl of yours that got shot? "Serves her right for being out there."

The world stopped. For Seth, it was like watching a star collapse. The man who stood beside him was no longer his compassionate, doting father. He was an architect of ruin, an ancient force of retribution awakened by a fool's careless words. David didn't even blink. He simply ceased to be the man he was a second before.

The shift from absolute stillness to kinetic violence was so instantaneous it seemed to break the laws of physics. There was no lunge, no preparatory tensing of muscles. One moment, David stood beside the flimsy wooden table. The next, his hands were on Hector. Not grasping, but encompassing. His left hand cupped the back of Hector's skull, the right clamped over his face, thumb and forefinger digging into the sockets of his eyes.

Hector didn't even have time to scream. There was only a single, hideous, wet crunch. The sound of a rotten gourd being stepped on. The sound of a skull collapsing under pressure far beyond its design tolerance. David released him, and Hector slid from his chair like a boneless sack of meat, his head a ruined, misshapen thing.

Silence reigned for a nanosecond, a collective gasp of disbelief from the other five men. That was all the time Seth needed. While all eyes were on the impossible event of Hector's death, Seth's gaze had darted to the table. His hand shot out, snatching a greasy dinner fork.

The younger guard, the one who had stammered about the pigs, was fumbling to unsling the rifle from his shoulder. He was too slow. Seth moved inside the weapon's arc, his motion a blur of inherited fury. He slammed the guard against the wall, his left hand grabbing a fistful of shirt while his right drove the fork into the soft flesh of the man's throat. He didn't just stab. He raked, tearing sideways with all his strength. A spray of arterial red painted the grimy wall as the man gargled his last, astonished breath.

Seth pivoted instantly. The second guard was frozen, staring at Hector's body. He never saw Seth coming. The same fork, dripping and grotesque, found its home in his neck. Another brutal tear, and he collapsed, clutching at the wound as his life poured out onto the dusty floorboards. Two seconds had passed. Three men were dead.

The remaining three men snapped out of their stupor. One, a burly man with a gut spilling over his belt, let out a terrified bellow and grabbed the only weapon within reach: a wooden baseball bat leaning against the wall. He swung it with all his might, a desperate, wild arc aimed at David's head. David didn't dodge. He didn't even flinch. He simply raised his right forearm to intercept the blow.

The impact was not the dull thud of wood against flesh. It was a sharp, explosive CRACK as the solid ash bat shattered against David's arm, splintering into a dozen pieces. The man stumbled back, his eyes wide with animal terror, staring at the useless handle still clutched in his hand, then at David's unblemished arm. He had hit a man with a baseball bat and the bat had lost. The fundamental rules of his world had just been rewritten, and he was on the wrong side of the equation.

Behind him, his two remaining companions were scrambling for purchase on a reality that had just been torn to shreds. One fumbled for a pistol tucked into his waistband; the other simply began to back away, his hands raised in a universal gesture of surrender. David sighed, a sound of mild disappointment, as if he'd been served a lukewarm meal. "Son," he said to the man with the bat handle, his voice calm and paternal, "you need a better bat." The man whimpered.

Seth, still vibrating, turned his attention to the man reaching for the pistol. The bloody fork still in his hand. "Dad, I'm going to take his head off." David's hand, large and steady, landed gently on Seth's shoulder "Easy, son. Let him make his choice." The man's hand froze, hovering over the grip of his gun. He looked from David's placid, almost bored expression to Seth's feral glare. He saw the bodies of his friends on the floor, one with his skull caved in, two decorated with cheap cutlery. He saw the shattered bat. He made his choice. Very slowly, he raised his empty hands. The last man, already backing away, bumped into the wall and slid to the floor, curling into a fetal position.

The synchronized thwip-thwip-crack of three suppressed rifles echoed from outside, Noah's .338 Lapua, Elena's .308, and Lily's .300 Win Mag speaking in a single, deadly syllable. It was the all-clear. The front door swung open and Lily stepped inside, her two short swords sheathed on her back and her father's wakizashi and Beretta held carefully in one hand, Seth's knives in the other. She took in the scene with the practiced eye of a professional assessing a messy job site. Her gaze flickered over Hector's rearranged skull, the two fork victims, and the three terrified survivors. She looked at Seth, who was still breathing heavily, his knuckles white around the bloody utensil.

"Dad," she said, her tone the one a daughter uses upon discovering her father has been 'fixing' the plumbing again. "You made a mess." She handed him his weapons. "Seth, nice work with the… fork." Darrel walked in beside Emma, his kamas riding high on his back. He took in the scene with a practiced, almost professional detachment. David and Seth looked like they'd just finished enthusiastically butchering a hog with insufficient tools. Blood spattered across David's face and soaked the front of Seth's shirt. Three men remained, two standing in abject terror, one a whimpering ball on the floor. Emma's hand went to her mouth, her eyes wide, but she said nothing.

Darrel, however, simply arched an eyebrow. His gaze drifted from the fork still clutched in Seth's hand to the man whose head now resembled a burst melon. "Well," he drawled, "that's one way to get your daily serving of iron." Suddenly, the man who had been fumbling for his pistol swayed on his feet. A wet, gurgling sound escaped his throat, and he doubled over, violently vomiting down the front of his own shirt and onto the floor. The stench of bile and terror filled the small room, layering itself over the coppery tang of blood.

Darrel just shook his head slowly, a faint, weary smile playing on his lips. Emma glanced at him, a questioning look on her face. Lily wrinkled her nose. "Seriously? As if this wasn't enough of a mess." "You know," Darrel said thoughtfully, addressing no one in particular, "for future reference, I think we've discovered a universal reaction to… let's call it 'creative dismemberment.' Seems like seeing a man turned into a modern art installation has a powerful emetic effect."

David, wiping a smear of blood from his cheek with the back of his hand, gave a low chuckle that seemed to rumble up from the center of the earth. He took his wakizashi and Beretta from Lily. He handed Seth his throwing knives, then placed a heavy, steadying hand back on his son's shoulder. "Seth. Outside. Go find Junior and get some water."

Seth nodded mutely, his adrenaline crash beginning. He looked down at the fork in his hand as if seeing it for the first time, dropped it with a clatter, and stumbled out the door without a word. "Emma, stay with Lily," David commanded softly. "Darrel, with me." He turned his placid, almost sleepy eyes toward the two remaining conscious men. The one who hadn't thrown up was trembling so hard his teeth chattered. "Lily, tie their hands. Use the zip ties from your pack."

Lily moved swiftly pulling a bundle of heavy-duty zip ties from a pouch on her belt. "Don't get any of that on you, Darrel," she advised, gesturing with her chin toward the puddle of vomit. "It's a pain to wash out." Just as Lily cinched the first tie, Junior appeared in the doorway. He was immaculate, not a speck of dust or blood on him. His eyes swept the room in a single, comprehensive glance: the bodies, the prisoners, the blood on his father, and the look on Emma's face. A silent conversation passed between him and David in less than a second.

"All clear out here, Dad," Junior reported, his voice low and even. "Perimeter's secure. Riley and Parker have eyes on the second house. No movement." He stepped inside, his presence filling the room. "Seth's with Andrew. He's washing off the blood." "Good," David replied simply. He took a step closer to the men, who flinched as if he were a lightning strike. He crouched down, bringing himself to eye level with the one who'd puked. The man smelled foul, but David didn't react. His voice was no longer paternal or amused. It was as flat and hard as bedrock.

"Now," he began, "we're going to have a little chat. About nine years ago, my family and I settled on a ranch about five miles west of here. We've bothered no one. Yesterday, someone put a bullet through my future son-in-law and into my daughter. A 7.62x39 round, to be exact."

He paused, letting the silence stretch. "Your friends out there," he gestured vaguely toward the bodies, "had AK-pattern rifles. So do the men we can see in the next compound over. So, you're going to tell me who pulled the trigger. You're

73

going to tell me everything about your little community here. And you're going to do it now." He glanced at Darrel. "Because my friend Darrel gets very creative when he's bored. And let me tell you," David's eyes crinkled in a terrifyingly pleasant smile, "you do not want to see what he can do with a pair of kamas and a roll of duct tape."

Chapter 29:

The Foreshadowed Rival

The man who had vomited let out a choked whimper, his eyes wild with terror as they flicked between David's cold, patient stare and Darrel's gleaming, whirling blade. "We don't know who pulled the trigger!" he blurted out, the words tumbling over each other in a desperate torrent. "I swear! We just... we heard the shot yesterday afternoon. Went to check it out. The trap was sprung, the pigs were right there for the taking!" He squeezed his eyes shut. "Eli, our boss, he said it was a gift. We just butchered them. We all got a share of the meat, that's it! That's all I know!"

David remained crouched, his expression unchanging. Junior stood like a statue in the doorway, his arms crossed over his chest. Emma, standing slightly behind him, rested a hand on his back, her knuckles white. She was seeing a side of this life, and of the man her father-in-law was, that she had previously only heard about from stories. It was one thing to hear about Junior ripping a man apart; it was another to see the man who raised him calmly orchestrate this chilling interrogation after crushing a man's skull.

Suddenly, a different prisoner, an older man with a wiry, salt-and-pepper beard, spoke up. His voice was a dry rasp. "He's telling the truth," he said, pushing himself up to sit straighter against the wall. "We're just muscle. The man you need to talk to is Eli, Eli." David's head tilted a fraction of an inch, his focus shifting to the new speaker.

The older man saw his opening and took it. "He owns it all. This house, the one next door, the big one on the hill. All of it. He had it all set up years before the blackout. Barricades, supplies, generators… everything. Told us it was coming. Said he had a… a vision. Knew it was all going to happen."

Darrel froze mid-twirl, the kama held perfectly still in his hand. His witty facade dropped, replaced by a look of dawning, incredulous realization. He slowly lowered his weapon, his eyes wide as he looked from the prisoner to David. "Now hold on just a damn minute," Darrel said, his voice dropping its playful tone for one of genuine shock. "Prepared for years? Had a vision?" He took a step closer to David, his voice a conspiratorial whisper that still carried through the quiet room. "Boss… you don't think this Eli fella is another one of… you, do you?" He gestured between the prisoner and David. "Like, another guy who got the apocalypse syllabus before the final exam?"

The air in the room changed. Junior's head snapped toward his father, the tactical implications of a hostile with David's preternatural knowledge flooding his mind. It wasn't just a rival gang leader; it was a rival intellect, a rival strategist, potentially with the same physical enhancements. Lily, having finished securing the last man, stood and looked at her father, her usual combat focus replaced by profound curiosity. This was a variable they hoped they'd never have to face.

David's gaze, which had been fixed on the now-silent prisoner, shifted slowly to Darrel. The patriarch's face was an unreadable mask, but a flicker of something, surprise, perhaps, or even a strange sort of validation, danced in his dark eyes. The concept, which he had privately considered a solitary burden, was now spoken aloud in the dusty air of this stranger's house. He wasn't alone. The thought was both terrifying and, in a bizarre way, comforting.

He let the silence hang for a moment longer, allowing the full weight of Darrel's question to settle on everyone. Junior's hand, which had been resting on the grip of his X-Ten, tightened imperceptibly. Lily's sharp eyes darted between her father and the prisoner, her mind racing, calculating the odds of a foe who could anticipate their every move.

Finally, David's attention snapped back to the terrified man on the floor. "The apocalypse syllabus," he mused, a ghost of a smile touching his lips. "An interesting way to put it." He took a single, deliberate step forward, his shadow falling over the prisoner. "Yesterday," David said, his tone leaving no room for lies, "two of my family were shot near a pig trap east of here. A man and a girl. The girl is dying. They were hit with a 7.62x39. Was it Eli's order?"

The prisoner, who had been shrinking under the combined gazes of the deadliest people he'd ever seen, began shaking his head so violently it seemed it might come loose. "No! No, sir, I swear it wasn't!" he stammered, his eyes wide with genuine panic. "Eli would never... that's not his way!

That kind of thing, shooting people unprovoked… it brings the wrong kind of attention. It brings… well, it brings you."

Junior exchanged a look with Lily. The man's logic was sound. An unprovoked attack was a declaration of war, and a leader with foreknowledge would understand that better than anyone. It was a stupid move, and whatever else this Eli was, he didn't sound stupid. "Explain his 'way'," David commanded, his voice patient but lined with steel.

"He… he doesn't govern us, not really," the man rushed to explain, desperate to make them understand. "Look, Eli is… Eli is a survivalist. He's about your age, maybe a little older. Has a wife, a couple of kids. He keeps to himself up in that big house on the hill. The deal is simple: we live here, on his land, and in exchange, we act as a buffer. We guard the perimeter, we watch the approaches. We protect his home. As long as his family is safe and nobody brings an army to his door, he doesn't care what we do. He wants to be left alone to ride it out with his family. That's it. That's the whole deal."

Darrel, having holstered his kamas, leaned against a doorframe, folding his arms. "So he's less of a king and more of a landlord with a heavily armed homeowners association," he quipped, the tension having eased just enough for his wit to resurface. "But if he doesn't govern you," Lily interjected, her voice sharp and analytical, "then who's to say one of your people didn't get trigger-happy on their own? Who in this settlement uses an AK or an SKS?" The prisoner's face paled. He swallowed hard, his eyes darting toward the door as if he could will himself to be anywhere else. "A few of the guys…

a lot of them. It's a common round. Easy to find. But Eli wouldn't approve. If he found out someone drew this kind of heat on us, he'd... he'd handle it."

David processed this new information. An intellectual and possibly physical equal who wasn't a megalomaniac, but a reclusive family man. A man who had the same incredible gift but had chosen to use it solely for the protection of his own, creating a buffer of expendable people to shield himself from the chaos. It was a completely different approach from David's own.

"So, to be clear," David said, his voice dropping into a conversational tone that was somehow more menacing than his commands, "you're telling me that your leader is a man who knew the world was ending, fortified his home, surrounded himself with lesser men to act as meat shields, and now claims no responsibility when one of those shields decides to start shooting kids for sport?" The prisoner flinched. "I... when you put it like that..."

David's expression softened. He was intrigued. This Eli was a new chess piece on a board David thought he had completely mapped out. An unexpected variable. He clapped his hands together once, a sharp, decisive sound. "Alright. I want to talk to this man." The statement was so matter-of-fact, so utterly devoid of the menace of their current situation, that it took everyone a moment to process.

Darrel pushed off the doorframe. "Whoa, whoa, hold the phone. You want to just stroll up to the Landlord of Doom's front door and have a chat? After we just dismantled his heavily armed tenant's association and turned their leader's head into a cantaloupe?" "Essentially, yes," David said with a pleasant nod. He turned to the prisoner. "You're going to be our ambassador. Our white flag, if you will." The man's face went from pale to ghostly. "Me? No, man, you can't. Eli... he doesn't do visitors. Especially not visitors who just... did all this." He gestured vaguely at the carnage.

It was Emma who voiced the group's tactical concern. She looked at her husband, her brow furrowed with genuine worry. "Junior, is that really a good idea? David," she said, turning her gaze to the patriarch, "this man has had the same twenty-five years you have. He knows what's coming. He's probably anticipated an approach like this. The path to his house could be a kill box. He's prepared for anything." A brief silence followed Emma's logical and sobering assessment. She was right. An equal intelligence with the same foreknowledge would be the most dangerous foe they could possibly face.

Then Lily stepped forward. She didn't look at David, but at Emma, her expression, educational, as if explaining a fundamental law of physics. "Emma, that's where you're wrong," Lily began, her voice calm. "We just broke Eli's first perimeter without a scratch. This," she swept a hand around the chaotic, blood-stained house, "was his early warning system, and we walked through it like it was a screen door. You know what happens when someone gets within a mile of our ranch? They take a dirt nap. Seth or Noah would have a bullet in their brain before they even knew they were spotted. That's the first difference."

She took another step, her presence commanding the room. "The second, and most important, is the difference in thinking. Eli planned to survive the apocalypse. It's a simple way of thinking for a survivalist. You build a deep bunker, you hoard food, you put up walls, and you hide behind them. He built a fortress to weather the storm."

Lily paused, letting her words sink in before delivering the final, crushing point. "My father," she said, her voice ringing with absolute conviction, "didn't prepare his family to survive an apocalypse. He prepared us for a future beyond it. He didn't build a bunker; he built a dynasty. He didn't hoard supplies; he cultivated strength. Eli surrounded himself with expendable men, with meat shields like this guy. Dad surrounded himself with us."

She leveled a gaze at Emma that was both reassuring and terrifyingly certain. "Eli's plan is finite. Ours is generational. Even his strongest, most loyal, hand-picked follower, his very best man, probably couldn't compete with Bonnie." As the tension eased, Noah approached Seth. He handed him back his M4 with a curt nod. "Looks like you had fun in there." Seth took the rifle, his cheeks burning slightly. "Thanks, Noah. Appreciate it."

Their ne guide looked back toward the house. "What... what about the other two inside? Are you going to... to kill them?" David, who had been calmly surveying the scene, turned his unnerving gaze on the man. The prisoner recoiled as if struck. "Do you think they will be a problem?" David asked. The man stammered, "No... no, sir. They're... they're scared shitless. They wouldn't dare cause any trouble."

David's lips twitched in a smile. "Lily," he said. "Bring the other two men out here immediately." Lily simply nodded and disappeared back into the house. Moments later, she emerged, flanking two more men even more terrified than the first. They stumbled forward, their eyes darting around the scene.

David gestured towards the house. "You two," he said, his voice leaving no room for argument. "Clean this mess. You need to bury the dead, deep. And wait for our return. Do you understand?" The two men nodded frantically, their faces pale. "Yes! Yes, sir! Anything you say! We understand!"

Their new guide, a man whose swagger had evaporated into a puddle of pure fear, looked at the group surrounding him. He'd counted five, maybe six when the chaos finally stopped. He was wrong. So catastrophically wrong. As if summoned by his thoughts, the world around him began to shift. A whisper of movement from behind a rusted-out pickup resolved into Josh, his M4 held at a low ready, and Caleb, his face a grim mask. From a dense thicket of mesquite that the guide would have sworn was empty, Riley appeared, her sarcastic smirk firmly in place, followed by a watchful Andrew. From a shallow ditch to his left, Scott and Parker rose like specters, as if they materialized from the earth itself. On the right, Reagan emerged from behind a dilapidated shed, with Marvin a step behind her. Finally, Elena stepped out from her sniper's hide, her Ruger 308 nuzzled in the crook of her arm.

The man's jaw went slack. His gaze swept across the assembled force, a ghost platoon that had materialized from the heat shimmer and the Texas scrub. They were a walking armory, each member moving with a predatory grace. He saw pistols, rifles, even the wicked gleam of edged weapons. He counted. Ten… eleven… fourteen people. Not counting the boy, Seth. Fifteen. And the snipers who had dropped his men outside were among them. They hadn't been attacked by a desperate raiding party. They had been systematically dismantled by a small, professional army. The realization settled in his gut like a cold stone: they had never, not for a single second, stood a chance.

He swallowed hard, his throat dry as dust. His eyes found David, the calm center of this hurricane of lethality. Spurred by a desperate need to understand the logic of the man who now held his life in his hands, he croaked, "Why? Why make them bury the dead?" He expected an answer about dominance, about breaking their spirits, about rubbing their noses in their defeat.

David looked at him, a flicker of something unreadable in his eyes. "To prevent disease," he said simply. "Flies will be on those bodies in an hour. They carry filth. That filth gets in your water, on your food. Then comes dysentery, cholera. You still have to live here. It's for your own safety."

As David's people reformed their lines, the transition was seamless, a fluid dance of lethal purpose. The three teams fell into formation with the quiet efficiency of a well-drilled unit, yet they lacked the stiff formality of soldiers. Jimmy watched the witty one, Darrel, affectionately teasing Reagan, who responded with an affectionate eye-roll. On the other flank, the country boy, Josh, shared a low murmur with Lily, who rested a hand on his arm. They looked less like a death squad and more like a large, heavily armed family on a particularly grim camping trip.

"Alright, let's move," David's voice rumbled, cutting through the haze. Stumbling slightly, his mind still reeling, the man fell into step beside David. The boy, Seth, walked on David's other side. They crested the small rise and began the trek across the parched landscape, the sun beating down on them relentlessly.

"Name?" David asked, his tone conversational, as if they were meeting at a town barbecue. "James," Jimmy croaked, his throat raw. "But... everyone calls me Jimmy." David gave a simple, accepting nod. "David." That was it. No title, no rank, no assertion of dominance.

Jimmy's mind, a frantic hamster on a wheel, kept returning to Eli. Eli, the leader of his settlement, was also a man who'd 'regressed', who remembered the world to come. But Eli was a fortress unto himself. He directed, he planned, he commanded from the safety of his reinforced farmhouse. He never got his hands dirty. He had people for that. People like Jimmy. People like Hector.

This man, David, was a contradiction. He was clearly the most dangerous individual Jimmy had ever seen, a force of nature in human form, yet here he was, on point, walking into potential ambushes, doing the grimmest work himself. It didn't make hierarchical sense. An asset that valuable shouldn't be risked on the front line.

He had to ask. The question bubbled up from a well of pure, baffled curiosity, momentarily overpowering his fear. He licked his chapped lips. "So," he began, his voice still a reedy rasp. "Back at your... ranch. Who's the boss? The one who calls the shots?" He expected the answer to be Junior, the formidable young man with the tomahawk who seemed to manage the group's combat operations, or maybe even Parker or Scott, the older, experienced-looking men. He figured David was the group's champion, their enforcer, the terrifying weapon they unleashed when things got ugly.

David's head tilted, a gesture of mild curiosity. A slow, easy smile touched his lips. "The family is," David replied, his voice a warm, pleasant baritone. "We all have our parts to play, little bits of a bigger puzzle." The answer felt like a riddle. The family? What kind of nonsensical, pre-apocalypse answer was that? In his world, in Eli's world, there was a boss, a chain of command, a pecking order enforced by violence and fear. This sounded like a platitude from a corporate retreat, not the operational structure of a kill squad. He risked a glance at the man. David didn't look a day over thirty, his features unlined by the stress and sun that had aged everyone else prematurely. Leaders were supposed to be burdened. This man looked like he was on vacation.

The rest of the party was converging, forming up with a practiced, silent efficiency that spoke of day to day life. They were a terrifyingly cohesive unit. Jimmy's eyes scanned their gear. Nearly everyone carried a black rifle, an M4 or something similar, and wore a tactical vest heavy with magazines, blades, and medical kits. They moved like a single, multi-limbed organism, each person anticipating the others' movements.

Then his eyes fell on the exceptions. David, the human blender, had no rifle. Just the sheathed wakizashi at his hip and the Beretta in its thigh holster. An executioner's tools, not a soldier's. He was the only one. It confirmed Jimmy's theory: David was the specialist, the weapon, not the wielder.

His gaze shifted to the man they called Junior, who seemed to be directing the tactical flow. That made more sense. Junior was flanked by two women, Emma and Riley. Both were armed and armored like the others, but something about their presentation was jarringly different. Around each of their necks was a delicate but unmistakable metal collar, gleaming dully in the morning sun. They stood close to Junior, their postures a study in deference, their eyes tracking his every move with a look of pure, unadulterated adoration.

When Junior murmured something to Emma and rested a hand briefly on her shoulder, she leaned into the touch with a reverence that made Jimmy's stomach clench. It wasn't fear; it was something else entirely. Worship. Jimmy's mind reeled. So, was Junior the leader, then? A charismatic cult leader with a pet monster named David? The group's hierarchy was becoming more confusing, not less. He couldn't reconcile the brutal efficiency with the strange, intimate social dynamics.

They walked in silence for several minutes, the only sounds the crunch of their boots on dry leaves and gravel and the distant caw of a crow. "This next settlement," David began, his tone maddeningly conversational, as if they were discussing the weather. "Tell me about them."

Jimmy swallowed hard, the dry click audible in the quiet. He had to be useful. He had to give them a reason to keep him alive. He dredged up the sanitized description Eli always used. "They're... resourceful," he said, his voice a hoarse whisper. "They have a unique, aggressive form of resource acquisition. They don't farm much. They don't have to." He hesitated, then added the part he knew would matter to a group like this. "They take what they want. From anyone."

"I see," David said, and a contented smile spread across his face, crinkling the corners of his eyes. "So they're bullies." He looked forward again, at the path ahead. "I hate bullies." The simple statement, delivered with such cheerful finality, was more chilling than any threat Jimmy had ever heard. He had a sudden, sinking feeling that the twenty-four residents of Settlement Two were about to have a very, very bad day. And he, Jimmy, was leading the apocalypse right to their door.

The ramshackle collection of buildings that constituted the second settlement gradually materialized through the thinning trees. It was a scar on the landscape, a haphazard jumble of prefabricated trailers, derelict RVs, and one larger, two-story structure that looked like it had been a small-town hardware store in another lifetime. A crude fence of corrugated tin, weathered plywood, and tangled barbed wire encircled the compound. It was designed more to keep people in than to keep threats out.

"Hold," David's voice was a low rumble that carried no further than necessary. "Cover and close." The command was executed immediately. As the main group melted into the tree line, four figures detached themselves from the formation without a word. Parker and Scott moved to the flanks. Caleb and Josh took up rear guard, their rifles held at a low ready. It was an instinctual dance, a display of unspoken trust and shared experience that left Jimmy gaping. They hadn't been told; they simply knew.

The rest of them gathered in a tight semicircle around David, who had pushed Jimmy down behind the trunk of a fallen pine. Junior crouched slightly, Emma and Riley resting their arms on his shoulders from behind. David didn't look at Jimmy. His eyes remained fixed on the compound, watching the lazy movements of a single guard pacing the roof of the hardware store. "Tell me everything," he said. "Don't sanitize it this time. Don't tell me about their 'resource acquisition'. Tell me what they do. Tell me what they have. Tell me who they are."

Jimmy's throat felt like sandpaper. He'd been here before, trading with others. He knew the stench of the place, the leering eyes, the palpable aggression that hung in the air like smoke. "They're scavengers," Jimmy began, his voice barely a whisper. "But not for parts. For stockpiles. They hit prepper caches, old storm shelters... places people thought were safe. They have a whole barn full of stolen food, medicine, ammunition. They don't plan, they just consume."

He licked his lips, the fear coiling in his gut. "They're armed. Well-armed. A mix of everything. ARs, AKs, shotguns. Whatever they've stolen. They're not trained, just... trigger-happy."

David nodded slowly. "And the people?" This was the part Jimmy dreaded. He glanced at the women in the group. "Twenty-one men," he stammered. "And... and at least three women, maybe more." Elena's head tilted, her dark eyes narrowing. "They have women fighting with them?" Jimmy shook his head, unable to meet her gaze. "No. Not fighting. They're... taken. From other groups. From families they've... broken. They keep them in the main building. They're mostly passed around, for... companionship."

Elena's face hardened. She stepped forward, placing a hand on David's arm. "Darling," she said, her voice laced with steel, "people like that don't deserve to breathe. They take what isn't theirs, they prey on the weak... punishment is the only language they understand."

Lily piped up. "Daddy, are we going to help those women?" David sighed. He hated situations like this. Innocence violated, lives shattered. He knew he couldn't just walk away, but the logistics of integrating traumatized people into their already complex community were daunting. "I don't want to leave them there, Peanut," he replied, "but I don't know what to do with them either."

"Dad, hold on a second." Junior interjected. "I need to put a pin in this right now before it goes any further." David furrowed his brow, confused. "A pin in what, son?" "In this," Junior said, his frustration palpable. "I hear you sighing over there, and I know where this is headed. Dad, I love you, you know I do, but I cannot take in any more wives. I am at capacity."

Jimmy's blood ran cold, a realization washing over him that was far more terrifying than the prospect of facing the settlement alone. The man with the placid expression and the blood of another on his hands wasn't an enforcer for 'The Family'. He wasn't a lieutenant taking orders from some distant Leader. This man was The Family. He was the patriarch, the father, the source from which all this terrifying competence and brutal efficiency flowed.

David turned his gaze back to Jimmy, the brief moment of levity gone, his eyes once again holding the weight of command. "You were telling us about the women." Jimmy swallowed hard, his throat clicking. His perspective had been irrevocably altered. He wasn't talking to an equal or a potential adversary anymore. He was talking to the man who held the lives of everyone here, including his own, in the palm of his hand. "What... what do they look like?" he stammered out, his own question feeling clumsy and foolish as soon as it left his lips.

Elena arched a perfectly sculpted eyebrow. "We were hoping you could tell us that, Jimmy." "Right. Sorry," he mumbled, feeling heat rise to his cheeks. "I... I only got a good look at one of them. A while back, on my last trade. They brought her out to serve us. Couldn't have been any older than her," he said, nodding his head towards Emma, who was now standing straight, her expression serious. "Young. Pretty,

I guess. Didn't speak a lick of English. She just kept her head down, fetched beers for everyone. Never made eye contact."

The description hung in the air, a grim portrait of subjugation. "Did you... engage their 'companionship' services?" Lily asked, her voice soft but with an edge of cold curiosity. Jimmy flinched as if struck. He shook his head vehemently, looking down at his own dirty hands. "No," he said, his voice thick with a shame he hadn't expected to feel. "First off, it was too expensive. They wanted a week's worth of food for an hour of 'company'. I don't have that kind of surplus." He paused, taking a ragged breath. "And besides... I had a little sister once. Before all this. I... I couldn't."

David nodded slowly, a flicker of understanding in his eyes. He respected honesty, even if it came from a corner of the apocalypse he'd rather avoid. He turned his head slightly, his gaze meeting Noah's. In rapid-fire Spanish, he murmured, "There might be something here for you, maybe." Noah, usually a man of few words, barely reacted, his face remaining impassive. But a slight widening of his eyes betrayed a flicker of interest.

David then shifted his focus to Seth, standing a few feet away, his youthful face a mask of stoicism. Speaking in fluid Arabic, he said, "It's time to begin operation wingman." Seth's expression didn't change, but a barely perceptible nod confirmed his understanding. He'd been briefed on all possible scenarios before they left the ranch; this was just another variable on the chaotic equation.

Jimmy, thoroughly lost, stared at them, bewildered. "What... what are you going to do?" he asked, his voice laced with apprehension. David's gaze returned to Jimmy, cold and unwavering. "We're going to kill them all." Elena pressed a kiss to David's cheek. "God, I fucking love you," she murmured, her voice deep with admiration and a touch of arousal. David simply nodded, his gaze already scanning the perimeter. He pulled Jimmy closer, speaking low enough for only the man to hear. "Keep some distance, Jimmy. You're about to get a promotion." Jimmy's eyes widened, his jaw slack. "Promotion? To... to what?"

Chapter 30:

The Sniper's Bride

David's gaze shifted from the trembling form of Jimmy to Noah. "Noah, the trees to the east," he commanded. "Find a perch with a clear view of the settlement's main gathering area. I want you to see every face." Noah gave a single nod. He didn't reply, he simply moved. One moment he was a solid presence beside Seth, the next he was a ghost, melting into the dense scrub and live oaks that bordered the trail. There was no sound of snapping twigs or rustling leaves, just his silent disappearance.

David then turned back to Jimmy, whose wide eyes were darting between the spot Noah had just vacated and David's unreadable face. David held out a pair of high-powered binoculars. "Go with him," he said. "Stay back, stay hidden, and watch. This is your first lesson in administration, Governor." He clapped a heavy hand on Jimmy's bony shoulder, and the man nearly buckled. "Governor?" Jimmy squeaked, the word a foreign object in his mouth. "But... I don't know anything about..." "You'll learn," David cut him off, his lips twitching into something that might have been a smile. "Lesson one: how to remove the opposition. Go."

Propelled by a fear more potent than any physical shove, Jimmy scurried after Noah, clutching the binoculars to his chest like a holy relic. As Jimmy vanished, Junior stepped forward. "Dad," he said, his voice a respectful baritone.

"Permission to execute a juggernaut breach?" A genuine, brief smile touched David's lips. He glanced at Elena, who was watching Junior with an appreciative glint in her eye. "A juggernaut breach," David mused aloud. "It's a bit dramatic for twenty-one scumbags and a handful of shacks, don't you think?" He paused, his eyes twinkling. "I like it. Proceed."

Junior's grin was feral. "You got it." David's head swiveled toward the right flank. "Josh! Twenty-five yards to the west, there's a small rise. You'll have a crossfire on Noah's position. Take Lily's Tikka." Josh nodded sharply. "Yes, sir." Lily turned to him, her expression softening instantly. She unslung the Tikka T3x. Then she handed it over to Josh without hesitation. As his hands took the rifle, she leaned in, cupping his jaw. "Don't you dare get a scratch on it," she murmured, her voice a low tease. "Wouldn't dream of it," Josh whispered back, his eyes locked on hers.

She pressed her lips to his, a kiss that was both a promise and a prayer, fierce and full of love. It was over in a second. She slapped his chest lightly. "Go." He gave her a final look and moved out, just as silent and efficient as Noah had been. Lily drew her blades, her expression once again becoming a mask of lethal focus as she scanned her team's sector.

Hidden in the trees, Jimmy had found a spot several feet below Noah's nest. He'd seen Josh's deployment, a mirror of their own. He raised the binoculars, his hands shaking so badly it took him a moment to steady the image. The settlement came into focus. Men lounged about, some brandishing AK-pattern rifles. They were lazy, arrogant, bloated with unearned power. Then he saw them. Three women, moving between the shacks, their shoulders slumped, their movements mechanical. One looked up, and even from this distance, Jimmy could see the utter vacancy in her eyes. The shame he'd felt earlier curdled into a hot, sick rage. His little sister... a wave of nausea hit him. He swallowed it down, his knuckles white on the binoculars. He was no longer just a terrified prisoner. He was a witness. He was... the Governor. The thought was still absurd, but now it held a sliver of purpose.

Back on the trail, Junior's voice was a low growl of command. "Team Two, stack on me. Riley, you're on my six. Emma, on her. Caleb, Andrew, Parker, file in. Tight formation. Watch your sectors." The team moved with practiced fluidity, a predator condensing its muscles before the pounce. They formed a tight, lethal column on the left side of the trail. On the right, Lily took point for Team Three, her movements impossibly graceful. Darrel, Reagan, Scott and Marvin fell in behind her, their faces grim and set.

David stood with Seth and Elena at the head of it all, the quiet epicenter of the storm. Elena rested her hand on his arm, her thumb stroking the hardened muscle. She leaned her head against his shoulder, her Ruger held casually in her other hand. "Operation Wingman is a go, I take it?" she murmured, referencing his earlier comment to Seth. David's gaze was fixed on the path ahead. "Seth is going to need a target to lock onto, and Noah needs a reason to be a hero." He gave the barest of nods, a signal that rippled down the line in a series of clicks as safeties were disengaged. "Let's go introduce them to the new management."

The world held its breath for a heartbeat. David's nod was less a command and more a release, like a finger slipping from a trigger. The potential energy coiled in Junior and Lily for the last ten minutes erupted into kinetic fury. They didn't run; they launched. Two blurs of motion, one a solid wall of muscle, the other a whipcord of deadly grace, devoured the distance to the settlement wall. The ground churned under their boots, their speed utterly inhuman, a sight that would have been comical if it weren't so terrifyingly real.

Up in his nest, Noah tracked their progress through his scope. He didn't need to. He could feel the shift in the air. He calmly swiveled his MRAD to the main building, his crosshairs settling on the forehead of a bored-looking man leaning against a sandbagged parapet, an AK hanging carelessly on his front. The man had just raised a hand to swat a fly from his nose. Thump. From Noah's position, it was a gentle push of recoil against his shoulder. On the parapet, the sentry's head vanished in a pink mist. He didn't fall; he simply ceased to exist from the neck up, his body slumping bonelessly a second later.

The sound of the shot was utterly swallowed by the cataclysm that followed. Junior and Lily hit the reinforced wall simultaneously. It wasn't a crash; it was a detonation. A sound like God slamming a car door echoed through the valley. Treated lumber, scrap metal, and rebar exploded inward, falling to the ground. A ten-foot section of the compound's primary defense was simply gone, replaced by a swirling cloud of dust and two figures standing silhouetted against the morning sun.

For a frozen moment, the lazy occupants of the compound just stared, their brains struggling to process the event. One man, holding a half-eaten can of soup, slowly lowered it. That was the last peaceful moment he would ever know. "Team Two, fan left, clear the shacks!" Junior's voice cut through the ringing in everyone's ears. His column surged through the breach, a perfect wedge. Riley was a shadow on his six, her M4 already sweeping, its muzzle a disciplined, deadly metronome. Emma, just behind her, moved with a fluid confidence that belied her submissive role; she was a predator guarding her mate's flank.

"Team Three, right flank, suppress the main building!" Lily's command was a silver chime in the chaos. Her team mirrored Junior's, a tide of retribution pouring into the compound. Darrel, his kamas held in a reverse grip, grinned. "Well, look at that. An original milled receiver Kalashnikov. Almost a shame to perforate the owner."

The compound erupted into panicked screaming and sporadic, unaimed gunfire. It was the frantic flailing of a kicked-over anthill. From the west, Josh's world was a series of pictures viewed through Lily's T3x. He saw a man in a filthy wife-beater raise his rifle towards Lily's team. Mine, Josh thought with a cold sense of ownership. A crackle of 300, and the man's chest blossomed red before he was thrown backwards into a stack of tires. He saw another scrambling for a weapon near a firepit. Another crackle. The man's scramble ended in a permanent, undignified heap.

From the east, Noah was the arbiter of fate. Target with RPK, aiming at Team Two lead. Problem. The MRAD thumped. Solution. A man trying to set up a machine gun on a barrel simply folded in on himself. Below him, Jimmy watched through the binoculars, his hands no longer shaking. He was cataloging it all, the swift, merciless efficiency. He saw the women, the slaves, dive for cover behind a water trough. He breathed a prayer for them.

On the ground, it was a meat grinder. Junior was a force of nature. He didn't just shoot. He slammed his X-Ten into one man's face, shattering bone, then used his forward momentum to bring his tomahawk around in a devastating arc, cleaving through the neck and shoulder of a second man trying to aim. A third man emptied a magazine in Junior's general direction. The bullets sparked and ricocheted off unseen armor as Junior closed the distance and simply drove a hand through the man's sternum. Riley and Emma provided a curtain of impossibly accurate fire, dropping two more men before they could even decide who to shoot at.

Lily was a different kind of horror. She was balletic. Her twin short swords were a silver whisper. A man charged her, screaming. She flowed under his clumsy bayonet thrust, one sword flashing up to sever his wrist, the other sliding cleanly between his ribs. She was already moving past him as he fell, his rifle clattering to the ground. Darrel, meanwhile, hooked one of his kamas around the leg of a rifleman, yanking him off-balance. As the man fell, Darrel's other kama sliced across his throat with a practiced flick. "Told you it was a shame," he quipped to Reagan, who was methodically putting two rounds into the chest of anyone still moving.

David, Elena, and Seth walked through the breach as if strolling onto their back porch. The main fight was already a foregone conclusion. Elena rested her head on David's shoulder for a moment, her Ruger held at a low ready. "They really should have read the Yelp reviews before setting up shop here," she murmured, her voice laced with amusement.

David's eyes scanned the chaos, not with alarm, but with the critical eye of a foreman. He saw Seth, his face a mask of cold focus. A large, bearded man, clearly one of the leaders, ignored the fighters and made a break for the cowering women, a long knife in his hand. David didn't shout. He just gave Seth a soft look. "Wingman."

Seth nodded once. He flowed forward, intercepting the man. He didn't use his knives. He didn't need to. As the man lunged, Seth sidestepped, grabbed the man's outstretched arm, and used his own momentum against him, twisting. There was a wet, wrenching pop as the man's shoulder and elbow dislocated in one brutal, fluid motion. The man howled, dropping the knife. Seth kicked it away, then drove his knee into the man's face with a sickening crunch.

The last of the sporadic gunfire died out. Twenty-one men lay dead or dying. The silence that followed was absolute, broken only by the whimpering of the wounded and the soft sobbing from behind the water trough.

The silence that descended was thick and heavy, tasting of copper and dust. It was punctuated only by the gurgling last breaths of the dying and the terrified, hitching sobs of the women huddled behind a large metal water trough. David surveyed the abattoir his family had created with a placid, almost bored expression. He gave Seth's work a nod of approval, the way a father might acknowledge a well-mown lawn. The man on the ground, whose face was now an unrecognizable ruin of bone and pulp, twitched one last time and was still. "Noah," David called over the radio. "Front and Center."

From the eastern tree line, a figure detached itself and began loping towards the center of the compound. Noah moved with an unnerving grace for a man carrying a rifle that was nearly as big as he was. He kept his MRAD at a low ready, his eyes scanning every shadow, every doorway, even though the fight was clearly over. Jimmy, the gaunt guide, scrambled down from the tree after him, looking awe struck and thankful to be alive.

As Noah approached, Junior's team emerged from a long, low-slung barracks on the left. Behind him, Emma and Riley moved with practiced efficiency, their rifles sweeping their designated sectors. Caleb and Andrew flanked them, forming a diamond as they escorted three more young women out into the oppressive sunlight. These were younger, barely out of their teens, their faces streaked with dirt and tears, their clothing simple and worn. They blinked against the brightness, flinching at the sight of the carnage.

Simultaneously, Lily's team cleared the main structure on the right. Lily stepped out, wiping her twin short swords on the pant leg of a dead man with a dancer's grace. "Clear," she called out, her voice crisp. Caleb was right behind her, his M4 covering their exit. Darrel flicked one of his kamas, throwing a spray of blood from the crescent blade.

Noah finally reached the command group, his boots silent in the dirt. He nodded to David, his eyes flicking from the mangled corpse at Seth's feet to the six women, three at the trough, three herded together by Emma. "David. Seth." David clapped Noah on the shoulder, a gesture of casual, absolute authority. His gaze drifted to the traumatized women, who were trying to make themselves as small as possible. The original three weren't looking up at all, their heads bowed as if in prayer or expectation of a blow. The three newcomers just stared with wide, vacant eyes.

"They've seen monsters for God knows how long," David said, his voice soft, almost a murmur. "Now they've just seen different monsters." He turned his full attention to Noah, his eyes crinkling at the corners in a warm, genuine smile that was utterly at odds with the scene around them. "Go help them, son. Be their hero."

As Noah processed the order, Jimmy shuffled cautiously from behind the cover of the main building. He kept his head down, his eyes fixed on the ground as if a single glance in the wrong direction might get him killed. He couldn't help but steal a look at the rescued women, though. His gaze fell upon one of the younger girls, the one with dark, wavy hair and eyes the color of old honey. He recognized her from before. He offered her a small, polite nod, a gesture of shared humanity, but the girl flinched violently, her head snapping down as if she'd been struck, a wave of shame washing over her.

Noah saw the exchange and felt a pang of something sharp and unfamiliar in his chest. A silent sniper's perch was his home; this was alien territory. He felt a nudge and looked over. Seth gave him a solid, enthusiastic thumbs-up, wiggling his eyebrows for emphasis. The sheer absurdity of it, a fifteen-year-old killing machine playing wingman in the middle of a massacre, was enough to break through Noah's professional shell.

A breath hitched in his throat. He was supposed to be a hero? He felt his hands twitch, wanting the familiar comfort of his rifle's stock. He glanced at David, who just maintained that knowing, patient smile. It wasn't a suggestion; it was an assignment. Taking a deep, centering breath, Noah squared his shoulders. He was a member of this family, and this was his part to play. He turned his head, his voice coming out a little rougher than he intended. "Riley, Emma… could you find them some water? Clean water, and maybe something to wash with."

The two women nodded without hesitation and moved to comply. "Darrel," Noah continued, feeling a sliver of confidence return. "Check the main building. See if you can find any clean clothes. Nothing fancy, just… something that's theirs, or at least clean." "On it, CasaNoah," Darrel quipped, heading back inside.

With the logistics in motion, the hardest part remained. Noah walked slowly toward the six women, his steps measured and non-threatening. He slung his rifle to his back, hiding it from view. He stopped a good ten feet away and slowly knelt in the dirt, bringing himself lower than them. The older women shuffled back, but the younger ones, including the girl Jimmy had nodded to, were frozen, watching him with terrified curiosity.

He cleared his throat, and in a soft, low voice, he began to speak, the Spanish feeling foreign but right on his tongue, his Tennessee accent coloring the words. "You're safe now," he began. Their heads snapped up at the sound of their language. It was like a splash of cold water. "We aren't going to hurt you. Those men... they can't hurt you anymore." He looked directly at the girl with the honey-colored eyes. Who was watching him, her lip trembling. "My name is Noah. What are your names?"

A long moment of silence passed, broken only by the distant caw of a crow. The women exchanged fearful, uncertain glances. Finally, one of the older women, her face a mask of hardship, whispered a name. "Maria." Then another. "Isabela." Noah nodded gently to each of them. He looked back to the younger girl. "And you?" he asked softly.

She looked at her hands, then back at his face, at the genuine kindness in his eyes that was so alien in this world. A single tear traced a clean path through the dirt on her cheek. "Mia," she whispered, her voice barely audible. A small, genuine smile touched Noah's lips. It wasn't the heroic, dashing smile of a storybook prince. It was the awkward, earnest smile of a quiet sniper from Tennessee, standing in a field of slaughter, trying to piece together a shattered world, one Spanish word at a time. And for the first time in a very long time, for Mia, it was enough.

Hours later, the brutal, chaotic symphony of combat had been replaced by the rhythmic, grim percussion of shovels hitting hard-packed earth. Outside the cleared cluster of shacks, Junior and Seth were excavating a hole large enough to be considered a municipal project. "You know," Seth grunted, pausing to wipe his brow with the back of a filthy glove, "for a guy who can rip a man in half, you'd think you could get this done by just punching the ground."

Junior didn't stop. "Keep digging, smart guy. These assholes aren't gonna bury themselves." "Technically," Seth mused, leaning on his shovel, his observant eyes scanning the work of the others dragging bodies, "they're not burying themselves now, either. We are. It's a bit of an existential conundrum, isn't it? Performing the last rites for men we just sent to their maker."

Junior finally stopped, planting his shovel and fixing Seth with a flat look. "The only conundrum here is why I'm digging a grave with a philosopher instead of another guy with a shovel. Less talking, more dirt-moving." He gestured with his chin toward the cluster of women, now huddled under the shade of a tattered awning, being watched over by a quiet Noah. "The sooner we're done, the sooner we can get them somewhere safe and our people home."

Near the shacks, the silence was of a different kind. It wasn't the quiet of work, but the fragile quiet of newfound, unbelievable safety. Noah sat on an overturned bucket, his MRAD rifle laid carefully beside him. He'd managed to get a canteen of clean water for the women, who sipped at it like frightened fawns. He had been speaking softly with Mia, his Tennessee-laced Spanish a strange, comforting balm in the wake of horror. He'd learned she was seventeen, that she and her family were from a small farm south of San Antonio before being taken. He learned her favorite color was blue, like the bluebonnets that used to cover the fields in spring. Small, human details that felt like anchors in a world adrift.

Isabela, Mia's aunt, watched him. Her face, etched with lines of terror and exhaustion, held a flicker of fierce, protective hope. She saw the bodies being dragged. She saw the pit being dug. She understood this was an ending, but she desperately needed to secure a beginning for Mia. Taking a shaky breath, she stood and walked toward the tall, imposing man who had directed the entire, terrifyingly efficient operation.

David stood like the calm eye of a hurricane, observing the cleanup. Elena stood near him, her rifle held at a casual low-ready, her gaze missing nothing. Isabela stopped a respectful distance away, her hands clasped so tightly her knuckles were white. "Señor," she began, her voice hoarse but firm, the Spanish tumbling out in a rush. "Please. My niece, Mia... she has suffered so much. She is just a girl. Is there some place... a safe place you would take her? Away from this. She will do as she's told, she will work hard, I swear it. Just save her."

David's gaze shifted from the grave-diggers to the desperate woman. His eyes held a flicker of something soft. He didn't look at her, but past her, toward the quiet sniper and the young girl. A slow, deliberate smile touched David's lips. It was a smile that held the weight of a past life and future plans. He answered her in the same flawless, unaccented Spanish. "Do not worry, ma'am. Of course we will keep her safe."

He then raised his voice, not shouting, but projecting with an effortless authority that cut through the sounds of the camp. His English was crisp and clear. "Noah." Noah's head snapped up, his conversation with Mia cut short. He'd been so focused he hadn't realized David was so close. "Sir?"

David gestured with his chin towards Mia, who was watching the exchange with wide, frightened eyes. "Isabela is concerned for her niece's safety," David announced, a current of amusement running beneath his dominant tone. "I've assured her that you will be personally taking care of her from now on."

The statement landed in the middle of the camp with the force of a grenade. Parker and Scott, hauling a body by its boots, both paused and looked over. On the right flank, Lily glanced at Josh, a grin spreading across her face. Over by the pit, Junior actually stopped digging and let out a short, sharp bark of a laugh.

Noah just stared. "Sir? I... I don't understand." David's smile widened. He looked at Noah as a man might look at a favored but slightly slow chess piece he'd just moved into a winning position. "It seems rather simple, son. The girl needs a protector. A guardian. You speak her language. You seem to have a rapport. You'll take care of her. Ensure she's safe, integrated. Fed. Cared for. It's a vital role."

Noah's gaze darted from David's all-knowing face, to Mia's hopeful but confused one, to Isabella's look of profound, soul-deep relief. His mind raced, trying to connect dots that weren't there. Why me? I'm just a sniper. I follow orders. This isn't an order, this is... a life sentence. A wonderful, terrifying, what-the-hell-is-happening life sentence.

And then he saw it. Across the compound, leaning on his shovel and trying very, very hard to look like he was fascinated by a clump of dirt, was Seth. He wasn't looking at him, but Noah could feel the smug satisfaction radiating off him like heat off the asphalt. He saw the barest twitch at the corner of Seth's mouth, the ghost of a triumphant smirk.

It all clicked into place with horrifying clarity. The long, quiet nights on watch. The hushed conversations with his young, observant partner. The times he'd idly mentioned, in a moment of vulnerability, that if this world ever settled down, he'd always hoped to find a kind, sweet girl to build a life with. Preferably a Latina, he'd admitted, reminded him of the good, family-focused people he'd known before the Fall.

Seth, David's son. Seth, the little spy, and a direct line to the patriarch. The kid had been on a reconnaissance mission. For him. Noah's jaw worked, but no sound came out. He had been outmaneuvered. Not by an enemy sniper or a tactical genius, but by a fifteen-year-old matchmaker with enhanced intelligence and a shovel. David hadn't just granted a rescued woman's request; he was nation-building, family-building, with the casual omnipotence of a god playing with toy soldiers. And he, Noah, the quiet man from Tennessee, had just been chosen. Promoted. Paired.

He finally looked at Mia. She was watching him, a single tear tracing a clean path through the dirt on her cheek, her honey-colored eyes filled not with fear anymore, but with a fragile, questioning hope. He'd come here to kill. And in the middle of a mass grave, covered in the filth of slaughter, David had just handed him a reason to live. He was going to have to kill Seth later. Affectionately, of course.

Jimmy, the gaunt newcomer, had been walking the perimeter with Caleb, his eyes wide at the scale and security of the team occupying the settlement. He'd seen David gesture, heard the Spanish exchange, and now he was witnessing the aftermath. He approached David cautiously, his voice a low, incredulous rasp. "Hey... boss?" Jimmy started, looking from Noah's petrified form to the women. "Did you just... did you just give that boy a wife?" Caleb, standing nearby, let out a short, soft laugh and shook his head. "First time?" he murmured to Jimmy, clapping him lightly on the shoulder.

David's smile didn't falter. He turned his gaze to Jimmy, his eyes warm and utterly devoid of doubt. "Jimmy," he said. "In the world before, men wasted their lives chasing status and money to earn the affection of a good woman. They forgot the basics." He gestured with his chin toward Noah, who still looked like he'd been struck by a non-lethal lightning bolt. "Noah is a good man. A protector. A provider. He deserves a chance at happiness. And that beautiful young woman," his eyes softened as he looked at Mia, "deserves to feel safe, to be cherished, and to be protected by a man who will lay down his life for her. I didn't give him a wife. I introduced a protector to someone who needs protecting. The rest is up to them, and God."

He said it with such simple, unshakeable conviction that it felt less like a social arrangement and more like a fundamental law of physics. Gravity. Thermodynamics. David's matchmaking. Isabella and Mia, of course, hadn't understood a word of the English exchange. But one word had sliced through the language barrier, landing with the force of a thunderclap: "Wife."

For Isabella, it was the answer to a prayer she hadn't even dared to form. After months of horror and degradation, this was a lifeline thrown from a battleship. Her survival instinct, honed to a razor's edge, immediately shifted from self-preservation to securing her niece's future. "Mija, mija, quickly," she whispered, her hands suddenly a blur of activity. She smoothed Mia's tangled hair, her thumbs wiping streaks of grime from the girl's high cheekbones. She straightened the collar of Mia's shirt, trying to make her look presentable, more than a victim.

She saw the women. These were not the broken, used women she had been forced to live among. They were warriors. They were family. Then her eyes landed back on the man David had chosen for her. Noah. He wasn't leering at her. He wasn't sizing her up like a piece of meat. He was part of this, this clan of clean, healthy, terrifyingly competent people who moved as one. To be attached to him was to be attached to them. This wasn't a sentence. It was a pardon. It was salvation. To deny it wouldn't just be foolish; it would be suicide.

With her aunt's firm hand on her back, Isabella gave her a push. "Go with him." Mia stumbled, her worn shoes catching on the uneven ground. She righted herself, her heart hammering against her ribs, not with fear, but with a wild, desperate resolve. Reaching out, her own smaller, dirt-smudged hands closed around his. His were warm, calloused, and felt shockingly solid, like anchors. He flinched at her touch, a jolt of electricity passing through him, finally breaking his stupor. His wide eyes snapped down to hers. They were filled with confusion, but not revulsion.

Mia took a deep breath, dredging up the few English words she'd gleaned from her captors. "My... Husband," she said, the words clumsy on her tongue but delivered with an unwavering conviction that transcended language. She tightened her grip on his hands, a silent plea and a promise all in one. "I... make you happy."

The spell was broken. A collective exhale seemed to pass through the group. Isabella, seeing the deal sealed, beamed with a relief so profound it nearly brought her to her knees. She stepped forward, released Mia's back, and on a surge of pure gratitude, rose on her tiptoes and planted a firm, motherly kiss on Noah's stunned cheek. He blinked, his brain officially overheating. Then, Isabella turned to David. She didn't bow or grovel. She looked him in the eye, a fellow survivor who understood the transaction that had just occurred, and extended her hand. David took it, his large palm engulfing hers.

"Gracias," she said, her voice thick with emotion. David's smile never wavered. It was the smile of a man who had just watched the sun rise exactly where he knew it would. He squeezed her hand gently, his gaze flickering from her to the new, petrified couple. "De nada," he rumbled, his voice warm and content. "He's a good boy. He will take care of her."

Noah, still holding Mia's hands as if they were the only things keeping him tethered to the earth, finally managed to form a thought. It wasn't eloquent or profound. It was just a simple, repeating loop of four words. Oh God, what now?

Chapter 31:

Under New Management

As if summoned by the shift in atmosphere, Junior and Seth emerged from the sparse tree line, their work done. The faint scent of freshly turned earth clung to them. They took in the tableau, Noah and Mia locked hand-in-hand, Isabella beaming at David, the other women clutching each other with a mixture of awe and relief, and paused. Junior raised an eyebrow, a silent question directed at his father.

David paid him no mind, his focus entirely on the women. His smile softened from one of smug satisfaction to genuine compassion. He turned to Lily and Elena. "The rifles from the dead. Check them. Make sure they're safe. Then give them to these ladies." Elena was already moving. She and Lily efficiently gathered the scavenged AR-15s, AK-variants and SKS rifles from the ground where the dead men had fallen. They worked with practiced ease, checking the chambers, clearing them, and ensuring the safeties were engaged before approaching Isabella and her group.

Isabella watched them come, her expression unreadable. Elena offered the first rifle, a worn but functional SKS, butt-first. "To protect yourselves," Elena said, her voice gentle. Elena and Lily finished their task, distributing the last of the scavenged rifles. Isabella held her SKS, testing its weight. It wasn't a gift; it was a tool, a transfer of power. She looked at the other women, her expression hardening with resolve. They were no longer victims. They were a garrison.

"Now," David said, his voice drawing everyone's attention. He spoke loud enough for all to hear, but his gaze was fixed on Isabella. He switched to Spanish. "This place... and the settlement a kilometer that way," he gestured vaguely with his chin, "are now connected. They are under my family's protection." Isabella listened intently, her brow furrowed. "Protection from whom?" "From anyone who isn't us," David replied simply. "You will be self-sufficient. We will not rule you, but we will protect you. A man from the first settlement, Jimmy, will act as your governor. He will ensure resources are shared fairly between both houses."

This gave Isabella pause, her suspicion flaring. A governor appointed by them? A man from another settlement? "Jimmy? Who is Jimmy?" "He's the gaunt fellow we brought with us," David glanced over at Jimmy, who stood near Parker, looking like a scarecrow that had just won the lottery. "A bit thin, but seems eager for a promotion. More importantly, he knows the area and he knows who Eli is." He turned back to Isabella. "There are two other men at the first house now. They are... cleaning. You and your women can stay here, or you can move to that house. Or you can split between the two. The choice is yours. This is your home now. Defend it."

As David spoke, Mia, who had been clinging to Noah's side, reached out and tugged her aunt's sleeve. She leaned in and whispered, her voice barely a breath. "Auntie, that man, Jimmy... he was already here. A few times, for provisions. He always had a kind look."

Isabella's gaze flickered back to Jimmy. She truly looked at him for the first time, not as an extension of these violent saviors, but as an individual. His gaunt physique, the hollows under his eyes, the way his clothes hung off his bony frame, it all screamed of prolonged hunger. He wasn't one of the well-fed captors; he was another kind of survivor, likely taken advantage of, given just enough scraps to remain useful. Mia's words painted the final stroke. Gentle eyes. A victim, not a predator. David's choice wasn't random; it was strategic.

Her posture softened almost imperceptibly. "And these other two men, the... Cleaners? Can we trust them?" "You can trust them to stay at the other house and mind their business," David said with a faint, wry smile. "They're sufficiently motivated to behave."

He scanned the faces of the women, then his own team. The sun was high and hot, and he was losing daylight. "We need to keep moving. We're going to the third settlement to have a talk with this Eli. But you are vulnerable here. Do you want me to leave someone with you? A guardian until we get back? It will probably only be a few hours." Isabella nodded immediately. The thought of being left alone, even armed, sent a fresh chill of fear through her. "Sí. Por favor."

Lily, feeling his gaze, straightened up from where she'd been checking the magazine on her P365. She met his look without hesitation. "Daddy, Josh and I can stay," she said, her voice clear and carrying. "The women will feel better with another woman here, and Josh can get the perimeter secured

114

properly while we wait." Josh, standing steadfast beside her, gave a single, affirmative nod. "We can handle it, sir. Keep 'em safe till you get back."

David gave a nearly imperceptible nod. "Good. Handle it." He turned his attention back to Jimmy, the gaunt guide. "You. With me. The rest of you, five-minute water and systems check. We move on my mark." The war party began to shift. Canteens were unclipped, weapons checked, and quiet words exchanged between fire teams.

As the others prepared, Isabella turned to her niece. Mia was still clutching Noah's arm, her wide, dark eyes darting between the formidable soldiers and the relative safety of the battered house. Isabella gently took her niece's hands. "My niece," she began, her voice a soft, urgent murmur in Spanish. "You have to go with him. This is your path now. You will be safe by his side." Tears welled in Mia's eyes, but she nodded. Noah, who had been listening quietly, offered her a small, gentle smile. He placed a reassuring hand on her shoulder. "Don't worry. I will take care of you."

Just as Mia took a step to follow Noah toward the departing group, Lily's voice cut through the air. "Hold up a sec!" Everyone paused. Lily strode over to Mia, a determined look on her face. To Josh's utter astonishment, she began unbuckling the straps on her own plate carrier. The advanced, lightweight armor was one of their most valuable assets. "She's not going with them unarmored," Lily stated, as if it were the most obvious thing in the world. She shrugged out of the vest and held it out to Mia. "This world's mean. No one should face it without a chance." She looked at Noah.

"Help her with this. It's fitted for me, but it's close enough to her size."

Darrel, leaning on his rifle nearby, let out a low whistle. "Well, that's one way to speed up the courtship process. Nothing says 'I'm committed' like providing mil-spec body armor on the first date." Reagan swatted his arm, but chuckled. As if deciding the state-of-the-art plate carrier wasn't enough, she unclipped the buckle of her gun belt. The heavy-duty nylon rig held her P365 in a Kydex holster, two spare magazines, and a small individual first aid kit. She offered the entire belt to the stunned girl.

"And this," Lily said, her voice firm but kind. "Armor's no good if the other guy gets the drop on you. Better to have the means to stop him first." Mia, who had been rescued from a nightmare only to be thrust into a bewildering new reality, stared at the plate carrier and gun belt as if they were alien artifacts. Her aunt, Isabella, recovered first. Her Spanish was a rapid, disbelieving whisper, her hands fluttering towards Lily before pulling back, not daring to touch the formidable young woman. "Miss Lily... are you sure? That is your armor. Your life. It's too big a gift for... for us." She looked at the advanced gear on her niece, a girl who, an hour ago, was property. The gesture was so profound, so impossibly generous, it defied comprehension.

Lily met Isabella's gaze, her expression softening. She switched to fluid Spanish, her tone losing its battlefield edge and gaining a familial warmth. "It's only a loan, ma'am. Think of it as a welcome to the family." She gave a small, confident shrug. "Mia will have her own gear soon. We can't have her running around with nothing. And don't you worry about me." She casually patted the hilts of the two short swords sheathed on her back. "I still have ways to defend myself."

Josh sidled up to Lily, wrapping an arm around her now unarmored waist. He leaned in and whispered, "God, I love you. You're gonna give my security-minded heart a full-blown panic attack, but damn, I love you." Lily leaned into him, her confidence unwavering. "She's with Noah. That makes her family. We protect family," she said, her voice soft but firm. She switched back to Spanish for Isabella's benefit. "He'll teach her. We all will. This is how we live."

David watched the entire exchange with a look of deep, paternal contentment. His daughter's altruism was a reflection of the world he was trying to build. He clapped his hands together once, the sound sharp and final. "A beautiful sentiment. Now, we have business with Eli." He turned his gaze to their captive guide, Jimmy, whose gaunt face was a mask of disbelief. "Jimmy-boy. Time for a little walk and talk. You'll be up front with me."

The group fell into their practiced formation with disciplined speed. David led the point team, his hand resting casually on the hilt of his wakizashi. He kept Jimmy just ahead of him, a human shield and guide all in one. Seth moved on David's right, his eyes constantly scanning, while Elena, her Ruger held at a low ready, flanked his left. Noah and Mia fell in just behind them. Mia walked stiffly, unused to the weight and bulk of the armor, her eyes darting around nervously. Noah stayed right beside her, a silent, reassuring presence.

As they began the 700-meter trek across the dusty, sun-baked terrain, Darrel fell into step beside Reagan on the right flank. He couldn't resist. "Okay, so let's recap the first date," he murmured, his voice low but carrying to the others in his team. "He says 'hi' in Spanish. She gets a full set of mil-spec body armor and a sidearm. What's the second date look like? A fully-customized AR? A crew-served weapon? Reagan rolled her eyes, but a grin tugged at her lips. "Behave. It was sweet."

"Sweet? That's the most aggressive act of courtship I've ever witnessed," Darrel shot back. "That's not 'I'd like to get to know you better.' That's 'I am contractually obligated to ensure you survive long enough for me to get to know you better.' It's romantic, in a terrifying, 'welcome to the apocalypse' kind of way."

Up front, David was ignoring the chatter from the flanks, his focus entirely on his guide. "So, Jimmy," he said, his tone deceptively casual. "This Eli fella. He a good man?" Jimmy flinched, sweat beading on his brow. "He's... he's in charge, sir. He keeps the peace." "Peace," David mused. "Funny word. The dead are at peace. Slaves are, for the most part, peaceful. It's not a word that impresses me much. Is he a fair man?"

"He... he makes sure everyone has food. Water," Jimmy stammered, his eyes fixed on the settlement now visible on a low rise ahead. It looked more organized than the others, with more permanent structures and what appeared to be actual defensive walls made of brick and mortar.

"So, he controls the food and water. And he has men with guns. And he calls it peace," David said, a hint of his signature wit coloring his tone. "Sounds like a government." He glanced back at Noah and Mia. The girl had stumbled on a loose rock, and Noah's hand shot out to steady her arm, his touch lingering for a second to ensure she had her balance. "See, Jimmy? That's what I'm a fan of. People looking out for people. Not because a man on a throne tells them to, but because it's the right thing to do. Does Eli do the right thing?" Jimmy didn't answer. He just swallowed hard, his Adam's apple bobbing in his thin throat.

As they closed the distance, the details of the third settlement became clearer. It was a small, self-contained ranch, built with more intention than the previous camps. There were guards on the walls, all armed with rifles. David held up a single, closed fist. Instantly, all fifteen of them froze, melting into whatever cover was available. The discipline was absolute. The sudden silence was more intimidating than a battle cry.

The effect was instantaneous and deeply unsettling for anyone who might have been watching. Fourteen heavily armed individuals, spread across a forty-five-yard front, simply ceased to exist. They didn't dive dramatically or scramble for position; they flowed like water into the landscape, becoming one with the sun-drenched scrub, the sparse trees, and the long shadows. The abrupt silence was a physical weight, broken only by the chirr of bugs and the frantic, shallow breathing of the man beside David.

He gave Jimmy a gentle, almost paternal pat on the shoulder that made the gaunt man jump. "Alright, Jimmy-boy. Showtime. You and me are going for a walk." "A-alone?" Jimmy squeaked, his eyes wide with terror. "Well, I wouldn't call it alone," David said. "I'll be there." He gave a slight, almost imperceptible nod to his left and right. "And my kids are watching. Now, chin up. Walk like you belong there." With that, David stepped out from behind the mesquite tree, his hands empty and held loosely at his sides. He ambled forward with the unhurried gait of a man heading home for lunch, forcing Jimmy to stumble along beside him.

From the wall, a voice called out, sharp and nervous. "That's close enough! State your business!" David stopped about fifteen yards from the heavy wooden gate. "Howdy!" he called back, his voice carrying easily in the still air. "Name's David! Me and my friend Jimmy here were just admiring your brickwork! Looking to speak with your boss, Eli!"

There was a pause. A head ducked down from the wall, shouting to someone below. Jimmy was visibly trembling, muttering prayers under his breath. "He doesn't see visitors!" the guard shouted back. "Oh, I think he'll see me," David replied cheerfully. "Tell him I've come about a personnel issue. An employee of his had a bit of an accident with company property yesterday. Fired a round that didn't belong to him. Tell Eli… I'm from corporate."

The absurdity of the statement in this dead world hung in the air. More frantic, muffled discussion from behind the wall. Jimmy looked like he might faint. David, meanwhile, looked up at the sun and squinted. "Hot one today. Be good to get in the shade." Finally, with a groan of protesting wood, the gate opened just enough for two men to pass through. A wary-looking man in his thirties, armed with an AR-15, jerked his head. "Eli's in the stable. Don't try anything." "Wouldn't dream of it," David said with a benevolent smile, stepping through the gate. He put his arm around Jimmy's shoulders, half-guiding, half-supporting him. "See, Jimmy? Hospitality. Now, which way to the horses?"

The interior was even more impressive. It was a functioning ranch, clean and orderly. People were tending gardens, mending tools, carrying water. There were children playing. It was a pocket of civilization, a testament to Eli's foresight. David took a deep, appreciative breath. "I like this. This is good work. This is worth protecting." Jimmy pointed a trembling finger toward a large, well-maintained barn. David nodded and steered them in that direction. The cool, earthy smell of hay, leather, and horse washed over them as they entered the shade of the stable.

Just as Jimmy had foretold, a man was there, rhythmically brushing the flank of a handsome bay mare. He was in his early fifties, with graying hair, weathered skin, and the tired, intelligent eyes of a man carrying a heavy burden. He looked up as they approached, his expression neutral but guarded. "You're Eli," David stated. The man put the brush down on a hay bale. "I am. And you're the man from 'corporate'," he said, his voice dry. "You can let my man go. He looks terrified."

David released his firm but gentle grip on Jimmy, patting the trembling man solidly on the shoulder. "See? I told you," David said, his voice warm and jovial, as if they'd just been invited in for iced tea. He leaned in conspiratorially towards Eli, though his voice was loud enough for Jimmy to hear clearly. "Jimmy and I have become fast friends. A real salt-of-the-earth kind of guy. You should give him a raise, Eli. Top-notch tour guide."

Jimmy looked from David's smiling face to Eli's stony expression and seemed to shrink in on himself, wishing the stable floor would swallow him whole. Eli's gaze remained fixed on David, dismissing the pleasantries and the terrified guide with a flick of his eyes. He recognized the type. Not the swagger of a common warlord puffed up on his own newfound power, but something else entirely. Something older, more settled, and infinitely more dangerous.

David returned the look, his smile never wavering. He let his gaze drift around the clean, organized stable, taking in the neat stacks of hay, the polished leather of the tack hanging on the walls, and the healthy sheen on the mare's coat. He reached out and stroked the horse's neck, the animal nickering softly and leaning into his touch. "Beautiful animal," David murmured appreciatively. "You've done well here. Very well. Clean water, livestock, security... a real bastion. It looks like you made good use of your twenty-five-year head start."

The words landed in the quiet stable with the force of a tornado. Jimmy, who had been trying to inch his way toward the door, froze completely. He didn't understand the meaning, but he felt the shift in the atmosphere. The temperature in the barn seemed to plummet. Eli's expression, however, did not change to shock or fear. Instead, a deep, profound weariness settled into his features, the look of a man who had long suspected a day like this might come and was simply tired of waiting for it. The guarded neutrality in his eyes was replaced by the dawning, grim light of understanding. He wasn't just facing a powerful survivor; he was facing a mirror.

"Jimmy," Eli said, his voice flat and devoid of emotion. "Go to the house. Tell Martha to serve you a plate of whatever's for lunch." The relief that washed over Jimmy was so absolute it was nearly a visible wave. He stammered a "Y-yes, sir, thank you, sir," and practically scurried out of the barn, not daring to look back at the two temporal anomalies who were now alone among the horses.

For a long moment, the only sounds were the soft swish of the mare's tail and the distant shouts of children playing outside. Eli broke the silence first, his voice low and resigned. "You knew. The 'corporate' line… it wasn't just a threat." "It was a professional courtesy," David corrected gently. "And an inside joke I suspected you'd appreciate. Why waste time with posturing? We don't have enough of it as it is, even with the second go-around." He finally turned his full attention from the horse to Eli. "So, why am I here?"

Eli gestured around the stable. "You tell me. You come to my home, bypass my guards with a riddle you know I'll solve, and dismiss my man like he's your own. You clearly hold all the cards, so why don't you just play them?" David's smile finally faded, replaced by a look of serene gravity. The shift was chilling. The witty, affectionate patriarch was gone, and the dominant, implacable leader stood in his place. He reached into the pocket of his pants, his movements slow and deliberate.

"Because this isn't a game," David said softly. He pulled his hand out and opened his palm. Resting in the center was a misshapen piece of metal, a lead and copper mushroom of violence. "This is about employee misconduct." He stepped forward and carefully placed the spent 7.62x39mm round into Eli's outstretched hand. Eli looked down at the bullet, his thumb rubbing over the warped metal. It felt heavy, not just with its own weight, but with the weight of consequence.

"Yesterday afternoon," David continued, his voice as calm and steady as a surgeon's report, "one of your people was northwest of here, near an old pig trap. He was carrying a weapon that fired this. An AK or an SKS. He got careless, or maybe he was just an asshole, I haven't decided which yet. He fired a shot. That shot went through the shoulder of one of my sons-in-law. A good man, a gunsmith. But the bullet didn't stop there." David paused, letting the silence hang. "It passed through him and struck my daughter. My fifteen-year-old daughter, Grace. This bullet tore through her arm, her ribs, her lung, and nearly reached her heart.

"My outposts... my patrols..." Eli started, his voice a low, strained whisper. "They don't just... let people walk through. How in God's name are you here?" David sighed, a sound more of weariness than exasperation, and leaned a hip against a hay bale. He picked up a loose piece of straw, examining it as if it held a fascinating secret. "Well, Eli, it was a busy morning. We had a series of very brief, very final exit interviews." He met Eli's gaze, his eyes holding no malice, only a profound sense of finality. "As of an hour ago, thirty-two of your... let's call them 'external employees'... are no longer with the company."

The number hung in the hot, dusty air of the barn. Thirty-two. Eli felt a cold dread seep into his bones. He had fifty-four people in total, including the sixteen here at his home base. David, with a force he couldn't even see, had just eliminated more than half his security detail without breaking a sweat. "Thirty-two," Eli repeated. "Give or take," David said with a slight, magnanimous shrug. "I'm not an accountant. My daughter Lily is better with numbers." He tossed the piece of straw aside. "At the first settlement, it was a personnel issue. Six men. We had a... disagreement.

They disagreed with living. We left two of their associates behind with strict instructions on sanitation and burial. A clean workplace is a safe workplace, after all. That's where we picked up Jimmy. He was much more amenable to a new management style." "And the second settlement?" Eli asked, almost afraid of the answer. "The one by the old quarry?"

David's expression tightened for the first time. The witty, detached corporate persona receded, replaced by a flicker of genuine, cold anger. "That one was different," he said, his voice losing its gentle cadence. "That wasn't a settlement, Eli. That was a pirate cove. A slave den. Twenty-one men, holding six women against their will. The youngest... a girl named Mia, couldn't be more than seventeen. Doesn't speak a word of English." He shook his head, a deep and profound disgust etched on his features. "I lived through this madness once before. I've seen the worst of what people become when the lights go out. But that... that's a special kind of filth. There are lines. They didn't just cross them; they paved a highway over them."

Eli felt a wave of nausea. "Slaves? My people were taking slaves?" He sank onto a nearby stool, the strength gone from his legs. He had set up those outer settlements as a buffer, a first line of defense. He gave them supplies, arms, and instructions to keep his core community safe. He hadn't visited them in over a year, trusting his chosen lieutenants to maintain order. He had assumed they were running things as he would. He had assumed wrong. "I... I didn't know. I swear to you, David, I had no idea."

David watched him, his gaze intense and analytical, searching for the lie. After a long moment, he seemed to find none. He nodded slowly. "I believe you," he said, his tone softening again. "You strike me as a builder, not a pimp. You're focused on the infrastructure, the long-term plan. You forgot the most important rule of management: you have to walk the floor. See what your employees are really doing when you're not looking."

He pushed himself off the hay bale and took a step closer, his presence filling the space between them. "Which brings us to our current situation. A hostile takeover, if you will. Or perhaps, a merger. Your outlying properties are now under new management, mine." He gestured vaguely to the world outside the barn. "I've left the five women we rescued there. They need food, shelter, protection. Things you will continue to provide."

Eli clenched the bullet in his hand. "Why not just take the properties?" David raised an eyebrow. "Why take it? Possession is nine-tenths of the law, Eli, and you already possess it. Running a ranch, even an off-grid one, is a damn chore. I've got my own spread to worry about, a family to feed, and a little girl with a hole in her lung. I don't need another headache, especially one populated by... well, let's just call them 'underperformers.'"

He paused. "Besides," he continued, lowering his voice slightly, "we're neighbors now. Sort of. Close enough that I can hear the distinct sound of your men getting creative with the Geneva Convention. And let me tell you, Eli, I hate killing the same people twice. It's boring. And it's a waste of perfectly good fertilizer." Eli swallowed hard. David's bluntness was disarming, terrifying, and oddly... refreshing. He'd been dealing with whispered anxieties and carefully constructed lies for so long, the raw honesty was like a slap in the face.

"So... you're just going to... what? Check in on us? Make sure we're not, uh, pimping out the livestock?" Eli asked, the question laced with a nervous levity. David chuckled. "Something like that. Think of it as a consulting gig. I'll provide guidance, training, maybe even a few free seminars on 'Ethical Post-Apocalyptic Resource Management.' I'll swing by every so often, make sure things are running smoothly, offer support where needed. You know, be a good neighbor. The kind that brings over cookies... and a small army."

Eli stared at him, utterly bewildered. "But... why? Why would you do this? You could just take everything, wipe us out, and add our resources to yours. What's the catch?" David's gaze drifted down to the bullet clutched in Eli's hand. He pointed at it with a casual, almost dismissive gesture. "That is the catch, Eli. Because you're going to give me the man that fired this bullet."

Eli's eyes widened. "You... you don't want anything else? Not our food stores? Not... not a percentage of our crops? A tribute? Jesus, David, you could bleed us dry, and we'd be hard-pressed to stop you!" David shook his head slowly, a genuine look of disinterest on his face. "Nope. Zip. Zilch. Nada. You keep your corn, your chickens, and your... questionable water purification methods. I'm not here for your stuff." He paused, letting the words sink in. "I'm here for the son of a bitch who shot my daughter."

Chapter 32:

The Consultant's Bargain

"So, tell me, David," Eli finally stammered, the name feeling foreign and wrong on his tongue. "What... what will you do with him? Once you... you have him?" David's gaze flickered, almost imperceptibly, towards the main gate. He took a slow, deliberate breath. "That, Eli, is not my decision to make."

Eli blinked, utterly lost. "But... you just said..." "I said I'm here for the man who shot my daughter," David clarified, his voice devoid of inflection. "And I am. But what happens to him after that... that's up to Grace." A wave of disbelief washed over Eli. "Grace? Your daughter? You're going to leave his fate in the hands of a child?"

"She's fifteen, Eli," David said, his voice softening, not in weakness, but in a weary understanding. "You have children, yes? Then you understand the gift you've given them. The knowledge, the... advantages. Grace is not just a child. She is the inheritor of everything I am, everything I've learned, every mistake I've made. She is, in many ways, more capable than I am. And this... this wound... it is hers to heal from, or to avenge."

He paused, letting the weight of his words settle. "Consider this, Eli. By taking this man, I would be robbing her of something. Of the chance to confront her own pain, her own anger. To decide for herself what justice looks like.

Do you understand?" Eli stared, mesmerized. He did understand, on a level that chilled him to the bone. He looked at the bullet in his hand, then back at David. "And what if... what if she decides she wants him dead?" Eli asked. David's gaze was unwavering. "Then he dies."

Eli swallowed hard. It was a simple, brutal equation. The kind that only someone who had seen too much, lived too long, could offer with such chilling detachment. "So," Eli began again, his voice laced with a newfound respect, "you... you've lived an eventful life, haven't you, David? More than once, it sounds like. And your... children. What are they capable of?" He gestured vaguely, trying to encompass the unsettling aura of power that seemed to radiate from David and, by extension, his unseen entourage.

David's eyes narrowed for a moment before softening. "I was a soldier, Eli. An interrogator, though that's a skill I also share with two of my wives. I was a chef, a swordsman, a mechanic. An artist, in my younger days. Archer, expert marksman... and, most importantly, a father."

Eli's eyes widened, struggling to keep up with the sheer breadth of David's experience. "And your children? They... inherit this? All of it?" David chuckled, a low rumble in his chest. "Pretty much. They know how to do everything I knew, but they've all grown beyond my own expectations."

Eli ran a trembling hand through his thinning hair. Clearly, he had miscalculated. He'd thought he was dealing with a survivor, a prepper who got lucky. Now he realized he was facing something... else entirely. A man who had, in a very real sense, prepared his entire existence for this very apocalypse. Not once, but twice, it seems.

David cleared his throat. "Look, I have a really big family, even grandchildren. The point is, this fuckwad almost took one from me. I figure, until she recovers, he needs to see the life he almost took. The family he almost took her from, and the people his bullet brought to your front door."

Eli's face contorted, a mixture of fear and resignation warring within him. "David, with all due respect... taking Thomas... he's not exactly a stable individual. He's... well, he's prone to outbursts. He regrets what happened, truly, but..." He trailed off, unsure how to adequately describe the simmering anger and paranoia that resided within Thomas.

David placed a hand on Eli's shoulder, his grip surprisingly gentle despite his immense strength. "Everyone regrets things, Eli. I've lived long enough to know that regret is a universal language. The alternative is letting someone else pay the price for his single mistake. But a dead man is a dead man; one less person making terrible mistakes." He paused, letting the weight of his words sink in. "However," he continued, his eyes twinkling with a hint of amusement, "turning the shooter into an ally can prevent a dozen terrible mistakes. Isn't that right, Eli?"

Eli swallowed again, his Adam's apple bobbing nervously. The implications of David's words crashed over him like a cold wave. He had envisioned David as a force of retribution, a righteous judge come to deliver punishment. Now, he was seeing a pragmatist, a strategist who viewed individuals not as inherently good or evil, but as potential assets or liabilities. And Thomas, the man who had jeopardized everything with a single stray bullet, was now being considered… an asset?

"But… but what if he tries something?" Eli stammered, picturing Thomas, armed and agitated, within the confines of David's ranch. "What if he's a danger to your… family?" "Eli, you worry too much," David chuckled, the sound surprisingly warm considering the circumstances. "My family can handle themselves. Besides, he won't be armed. And he'll be under constant supervision. Think of it as… an intensive rehabilitation program. With a generous helping of Texas hospitality."

He clapped Eli on the back, not quite hard enough to be painful, but enough to convey the seriousness beneath the jovial tone. "Now, about that gate…" Eli, thoroughly convinced he was dealing with a man who was either incredibly naive or possessed a level of confidence bordering on insanity, sighed. He knew when he was outmatched. "Alright, alright. I'll open the gate."

As the gate creaked open, the sight that greeted Eli almost made him slam it shut again. Fourteen figures stood just outside, a formidable tableau of weapons and grim determination. He recognized the calculated calm in their eyes, the kind that came from facing danger head-on and emerging victorious.

His gaze swept over the group, lingering on each individual. A young man with a wild look in his eyes, cradling an AR-10 like a lover. A woman with sharp features and a Ruger 308, her gaze unwavering. A teenager, barely more than a boy, his eyes darting around with unsettling awareness. And in the back, the longest rifle he'd seen in real life, carried by a placid looking man with a fiery red goatee.

Eli scurried towards the main house, his feet kicking up dust in his haste. He needed to find Thomas before David's…rehabilitation program…began. The thought of the fidgety, unpredictable Thomas under the 'generous hospitality' of that group made Eli's stomach churn.

Inside the main house, a nervous tension hung heavy in the air. The women were clustered together, whispering, while several of the men, Thomas included, stood near the windows, peering out at the approaching war party. "Thomas!" Eli called out, his voice cracking slightly. "I need to talk to you." Thomas, a lanky young man with perpetually greasy hair and a twitch, turned around. "What's going on, Eli? Who are those people?"

Eli grabbed Thomas by the arm and dragged him towards a quieter corner of the room. "It's…complicated. But the short version is, you're going to be going with them." Thomas's eyes widened. "Going where? I'm not going anywhere with those guys! Did you see the weapons they're carrying? They look like they're ready to start a war!" "Just listen!" Eli pleaded, sweat beading on his forehead. "They know it was you who shot that girl. But…they're not going to hurt you. David, the guy in charge, he says you're going to…help them out. At their place."

Thomas's face contorted in a mixture of fear and disbelief. "Help them out? You mean like…forced labor? I'm not a slave!" "No, no, it's not like that!" Eli insisted, though

133

he wasn't entirely sure himself. "It's…a learning opportunity! A chance to…redeem yourself!" Thomas scoffed. "Redeem myself? I was trying to protect us! That guy was getting in our way! That girl… she's our best shot at…well, you know." He trailed off, gesturing vaguely.

Eli massaged his temples. This was going exactly as badly as he'd feared. "Look, Thomas, just cooperate. Don't make things worse. Please. Just go with them, be polite, and maybe, just maybe, this will all blow over." He pushed Thomas towards the door, where David stood waiting patiently, like a benevolent but very, very large and heavily armed babysitter.

Eli all but shoved Thomas towards David, a silent prayer escaping his lips that the young man wouldn't do anything…stupid. Thomas stumbled, his eyes darting nervously between David's imposing frame and the armed figures visible beyond the open doorway. He swallowed hard, the twitch in his left eye intensifying. He was trapped, and he knew it. These people were not to be trifled with. David, a man who radiated an aura of quiet power, simply stood there, his face an unreadable mask. He waited patiently, allowing Thomas to absorb the gravity of the situation. He knew fear when he saw it, and Thomas was practically drowning in it.

Finally, David spoke, his voice a low, comforting rumble that somehow didn't quite reach Thomas's ears as such. "Well now, Thomas, isn't it? Seems you and I have a misunderstanding to clear up." He let the statement hang in the air. "I'm offering you two paths, son. Two choices. Both lead somewhere. But only one leads to a future you might actually enjoy."

"The first path," David continued, gesturing towards the open ranch gate, "is the path of cooperation. You come with us, willingly. You'll learn a thing or two about… apocalyptic etiquette, let's call it. See what life looks like when you nearly take it away. You'll work, you'll learn, and you'll contribute. My family isn't fond of slackers." He smiled, but it was a smile that didn't quite reach his steely blue eyes. "Think of it as a…an internship. A chance to see if your actions were worth the consequences."

Thomas stared at David, his mind reeling. This wasn't what he expected. He'd imagined anger, threats, maybe even immediate violence. This… this was almost worse. It was cold, calculated, and utterly terrifying in its rationality. David shifted his weight slightly and turned his gaze to the people behind Thomas in the settlement. "The second path," David said, his voice hardening, "is less…inviting. You stand here. You refuse. And my family and I will conclude that allowing this settlement to continue would be a threat to ours."

He leaned closer to Thomas, his voice dropping to a near whisper, audible only to him. "In that event, we will kill everyone in this settlement. Every man, woman, and child. Then, we'll dismember your body, and I'll let my family take pieces of your remains home as souvenirs." He straightened again, his face unreadable. "Consider it a… teaching moment. A reminder that actions have consequences, and some consequences are… permanent."

Thomas shuddered, his face paling. The casual, almost conversational tone in which David delivered the ultimatum was more terrifying than any screaming fit. He glanced back at the other residents of the settlement. Most were staring at the floor, avoiding eye contact, their faces etched with fear. Eli was wringing his hands, his eyes pleading.

He looked back at David. The man was an implacable wall. There was no arguing with him, no reasoning, no bargaining. There were only choices, and one of them led to oblivion for everyone he knew. He thought of the girl, lying injured. He hadn't meant to hurt her, not really. He just wanted to bring her here, without the other guy getting in the way. He'd been so focused on his goal, so convinced that he was doing what was necessary, that he hadn't considered the ramifications. Now, the ramifications were staring him in the face, armed to the teeth and ready to unleash hell.

He wanted to run, to hide, to disappear. But there was nowhere to go. These people would hunt him down, and they wouldn't hesitate. He could see it in their eyes. Finally, he swallowed his pride, his fear, and his resentment. He met David's gaze, his voice barely a whisper. "I... I'll go with you." David led Thomas away from Eli and the stables. The other members of the war party watched, their faces grim. Thomas, gaunt and pale, shuffled along, his eyes darting nervously.

David stopped a few feet away from Seth, who was standing ramrod straight, his jaw clenched. Without a word, David took the SKS from Thomas's trembling hands and offered it to Seth butt first. Seth's eyes burned into Thomas.

Rage simmered just beneath the surface, threatening to boil over. He took the rifle, his grip tightening until his knuckles turned white. "You shot my twin sister," Seth stated, his voice low and dangerous. Then, before anyone could react, Seth raised the rifle high above his head. A grunt of effort escaped his lips, and with a sickening crack, he brought it down, snapping the weapon in half, the wood splintering and the metal bending at unnatural angles.

The sound echoed through the settlement, silencing the nervous murmurs of the residents. They stared in disbelief, their eyes wide with a mixture of fear and awe. The casual destruction of a weapon that represented both safety and aggression, was a stark reminder of the forces they were dealing with. Seth dropped the broken pieces of the rifle at Thomas's feet, his gaze never leaving the man's face. "That's for Grace." He turned away, his shoulders rigid with suppressed anger.

David watched him go. "Now," David said, his voice calm and even, contrasting sharply with the violence that had just unfolded. "You owe Eli an apology." Thomas looked at David, confused. "An apology? For what?" "For forcing my family to kill thirty-two people to get to you." He gestured vaguely towards the distant horizon. "Thirty-two lives, all because of your selfish ambition. You put Eli's settlement, his people, at risk because you thought you could take what wasn't yours."

Thomas's eyes widened. Thirty-two people? He'd only thought he was trying to help his small town thrive. He had been so sure of himself. David leaned in, his voice dropping to a near whisper. "Eli took you in. Gave you shelter. And how did you repay him? By endangering everything he's built."

Thomas glanced at Eli, who was watching them, his face pale and drawn. Shame washed over him, a bitter tide of regret. He had been so blinded by his desire, so convinced of his own righteousness, that he hadn't seen the damage he was causing. He took a hesitant step towards Eli, his head bowed. "Eli... I'm sorry," he mumbled, his voice barely audible. "I... I messed up. I was wrong. I never should have done what I did."

Eli sighed, the sound heavy with disappointment. "Thomas," he said, his voice surprisingly steady. "Some of those... men, contributed to their own downfall. They were eager to fight, eager to take what wasn't theirs." He ran a hand through his thinning hair. "That doesn't excuse your actions, but it offers some... context."

He focused his gaze on Thomas, his eyes filled with a weary sadness. "Listen to David, Thomas. He's right. You endangered this whole community. Don't cause any more trouble. Cooperate with him. And... if that girl, Grace, is merciful, if she chooses to be, you might just come back from this a better man than the thirty-two we lost this morning." Eli turned away, dismissing Thomas with a wave of his hand. "Go. You're dismissed."

Left alone again with David, Thomas found himself completely adrift. He understood the apology, the need to acknowledge his wrongdoing to Eli. But David... David was something else entirely. He couldn't rationalize someone like

David. A man who possessed such obvious power, such terrifying efficiency, yet chose to lecture him, to offer him a chance at redemption. Why would he go through the trouble of teaching him a lesson? "I... I don't understand," Thomas stammered, his voice barely a whisper. "Why are you doing this? Why go to all the trouble?"

"The greater your fall," David began, his voice resonating with a quiet authority that demanded attention, "the more triumphant your climb." He paused. "I'm not doing this for you, Thomas. Though, frankly, your life has become something of a nuisance to me." A flicker of wry amusement crossed his lips. "I'm doing this for Eli, for his people, for the potential nestled within the ashes of your mistake. Your stupid mistake," he emphasized, his gaze unwavering, "may be the catalyst that makes you a good leader someday. Maybe."

David gestured around the settlement with a subtle wave of his hand. "Look around you, Thomas. Eli has built something here. Something sustainable. He cares for these people. He provides a haven. And you, blinded by ambition, nearly destroyed it all." He closed the distance between them, his presence suddenly looming. "Redemption isn't a gift, Thomas. It's a struggle. A constant, uphill battle against your own failings. You've taken the first step by apologizing to Eli. Now, the real work begins."

David's eyes softened, but only slightly. "You have the capacity for more than just selfish ambition. I see it, a glint of something resembling potential in your eyes. But potential is worthless without action. Without a willingness to learn, to atone, to earn forgiveness."

From the group outside, Parker chuckled softly, shaking his head in admiration. "He just made Eli's home a garrison," he murmured to Scott, who stood beside him, arms crossed, a knowing smirk playing on his lips. "And Thomas is now the most motivated pupil you'll ever see. Guarantee it." Nearby, Darrel nudged Reagan, his voice low. "I don't get it. Why not just…punish him? Make an example of him?" Reagan shrugged, equally perplexed. "That's what I thought. Simple, direct action. This…this is different."

Marvin, standing a few feet away, overheard their conversation. "Think about it," he chimed in, "An example for who? These people already feared David enough, he just took down thirty men, and made David's new friend look the other way doing it." Caleb, Riley, and Emma stood a little further away, listening intently. Caleb shook his head. "I thought for sure he'd just put him down." Riley, ever the cynic, raised an eyebrow. "David is never simple." Noah, speaking rapidly in Spanish to Mia, explained David's actions. His voice was barely audible, but his gestures were animated. "He has taken away Thomas's power…now Thomas answers to him and is in his debt." Mia listened with rapt attention, her dark eyes wide as she tried to grasp the nuances of this strange, powerful man.

Seth, standing near his father David, watched them all with an understanding beyond his years. He saw the confusion in Darrel and Reagan's eyes, the cynical curiosity in Riley's, and the budding comprehension in Emma's. He knew what his father was doing. He was planting a seed, cultivating a new kind of loyalty, forging a weapon out of guilt and regret.

David turned slightly towards Jimmy, his voice low and firm. "Jimmy, it's time to go. We have work to do." He gestured for the group to start moving back towards the second settlement. The walk was conducted in a loose formation, weapons at the low ready. Jimmy visibly relaxed as they moved away from Eli's farm and the tension that had permeated the air. He had been genuinely afraid of what David might do to Eli, or what Eli might do to him

As they walked, David spoke to Jimmy, his voice calm but carrying an undeniable weight of authority. "Jimmy, I'm putting you in charge of the outer settlements. That comes with a responsibility." He paused. "You need to ensure that people are treated fairly. That anyone who joins your community contributes. No freeloading, no taking advantage of others." David continued, his gaze fixed on the horizon. "There are plenty of supplies out there if you look hard enough. We don't need to steal from others. We need to build something better. Something sustainable. Something based on trust and mutual respect." He glanced sideways at Jimmy. "Can you do that?"

Jimmy, a nervous energy buzzing beneath his skin, swallowed hard. "I... I think so, David. I understand. But what about... what about people who genuinely need help? Folks who are sick, injured, can't pull their weight right away?" He looked at Thomas, walking a short distance behind them, his face etched with remorse.

David stopped walking, forcing the others to halt as well. His gaze swept over the group, settling on Jimmy with unsettling intensity. "The future has no room for weakness, Jimmy. This isn't about being cruel, it's about survival. We can't afford to carry the weight of those who refuse to help themselves. More people are going to die, we have to be decisive when it comes to deciding who we bring in to our community. Compassion has its place, but it can't be a death sentence."

He paused. "We can offer aid, teach skills, but if someone consistently leeches off the community, they become a liability. They drain resources that could be used for those who are willing to contribute. Understand?" Jimmy nodded slowly, the weight of David's words settling upon him. He understood the logic, the cold, hard mathematics of survival. But that didn't make it any easier.

As they crested a small rise, the second settlement came into view. Lily and Josh were waiting for them, standing near the newly repaired gate. Lily stepped forward to greet them with a weary smile, relief evident in her eyes. She scanned the group, her expression hardening as her gaze landed on Thomas. Lily's eyes narrowed, assessing the young man. "Who's this?" she asked, her voice sharp, suspicion coloring her tone.

David placed a hand on Lily's shoulder, a gesture of reassurance. "This is Thomas. He's going to be staying with us for a little bit. He made a mistake, a terrible one, but he's willing to make amends." He looked at Thomas, his expression firm. "He needs positive mentorship, Lily. Lily's gaze didn't soften, but she nodded slowly. "Alright," she said, her voice still guarded. "We'll see."

She turned to David, changing the subject abruptly. "What about Eli? What did you think?" David sighed softly. "Your assumptions were correct, Lily. The man is definitely waiting out the apocalypse, but he wasn't malicious. He had no idea what was going on here, so I told him I was taking over. I don't think he's a threat."

As David spoke, Thomas couldn't help but glance toward the edge of the settlement. The freshly turned earth and the unmistakable outline of a mass grave, however discreetly hidden, sent a shiver down his spine despite the oppressive heat. He swallowed hard, the reality of his actions and the sheer, unadulterated efficiency, bordering on ruthlessness, of David's methods crashed down on him. What in the ever-loving hell had he gotten himself into? He'd thought he was helping Eli's community. He was so, so wrong.

He took a tentative step forward, his voice cracking with nerves. "Lily... I... I need to apologize. For what I did. To Grace... to Kyle... to everyone." He stammered, searching for the right words, but finding only a jumbled mess of guilt and regret. "I never... I never meant to hurt her. I just... I messed up. Terribly." Lily listened, arms crossed, her expression unchanging. "Thomas," she began, her voice surprisingly gentle, "I appreciate the apology. And honestly, for my father's sake, I'll forgive you." She paused. "But I'm not the one you need to worry about."

Before the tension could thicken any further, David directed his attention to the five women; Isabella, Maria, Lucinda, Julieta, and Marina. "How are you, ladies? Are you all doing alright?" He asked, his tone warm and genuinely concerned. Isabella, the elder of the women, stepped forward, her face etched with weariness but also a newfound sense of hope. She answered David, her voice tinged with a grateful tremor. "We're tired, but so much better now, sir." She gestured to the others. "We still don't know what we're going to do."

David nodded understandingly. "Have you decided whether you will all stay here or if you prefer to split between the settlements?" Isabella hesitated, exchanging glances with the other women. Lucinda spoke up, her voice soft but firm. "We would prefer to stay together, if possible. It gives us more security."

David smiled reassuringly. "I understand. That is fine. You can stay here. This place will be your home now." He paused, his gaze sweeping over the settlement. "Eli will make sure you don't starve, and you will have the opportunity to make a home here." Then, turning back to the women, his expression turned slightly more serious. "However, I and my family will be visiting in the future, making sure everything is going well. Especially since Mia has family here."

He turned to Jimmy, who was standing awkwardly to the side, his eyes darting nervously between the women and David. "Jimmy, do you feel like you can work cooperatively with these women? This place needs to be rebuilt, and they deserve a good life after what they've been through." Jimmy swallowed hard, his gaunt face flushed. "Yes, Sir, I do. But... they don't speak English. How am I supposed to... you know... govern?"

David chuckled, a low rumble in his chest. "Jimmy, respect is a universal language. Treat them with dignity, listen to their concerns, and work with them to rebuild this place. Actions speak louder than words, after all. Show them you're here to help, and they'll understand." He clapped Jimmy on the shoulder, a gesture of encouragement. "You've got this. I have faith in you."

David clapped Jimmy on the shoulder one last time, the gesture meant to instill confidence, but Jimmy still looked like a stiff breeze could blow him over. "Alright, Jimmy, time to head back to the first settlement. David gestured towards Mia. "Noah, I expect you to start teaching Mia English. She needs to be able to communicate with the rest of us back at the ranch."

He turned back to the women, offering a final, reassuring smile. "We'll be back to check on you all soon. Don't hesitate to consolidate power and run the settlement as a group." As David turned to leave, Mia approached Lily hesitantly, her dark eyes filled with gratitude. She held out Lily's armor and gun belt, offering them back with a quiet "Gracias." Lily smiled warmly, accepting the gear. "De nada, Mia. I'm glad we could help." She turned slightly away from the group to slip back into her armor, the plates clicking softly as they settled into place.

Jimmy, shuffling awkwardly behind David, couldn't help but steal a glance at Lily as she adjusted the armor. It was hard to miss how perfectly it molded to her form, accentuating her curves in a way that seemed almost... bespoke. He'd seen plenty of scavenged armor in his time, but none of it had ever fit anyone quite so well. He gulped, trying to focus on David's back. "Oh my God, that armor is amazing." Mia, fluent in reading body language, noticed Jimmy's sideways glance and a knowing smile played on her lips. She understood the subtleties of male appreciation, especially after living in a place where women were commodities. The armor did look very good on Lily.

Once the initial awkwardness subsided, Mia's gaze traveled over the rest of the group, taking in their armor. It was fascinating. The soft armor worn underneath looked thin but comfortable, and the plates seemed to bend and flow around each person's physique. It wasn't like the clunky, ill-fitting scraps she'd seen worn by raiders and slavers. Even Noah's armor, designed for a sniper, seemed perfectly tailored to his movements, allowing him to stay low and concealed. Her brow furrowed slightly. Was this... custom-made?

Mia, walking beside Noah, tugged nervously at the hem of her borrowed dress. The rescue felt like a dream, especially after Isabella practically shoved her into Noah's arms, whispering about a "secure future." Now, she was walking amongst heavily armed people. "Noah," she started, "Am I really going to get my own armor?" Noah glanced down at her. His eyes. He spoke in slow, deliberate Spanish, "Si, Mia. David is very generous. You will get armor. Two sets, in fact. One for the summer, lighter and more breathable.

And another, heavier, for the winter months." Mia's eyes widened. Two sets of armor? It was unimaginable. "Two? But... why?" "To protect you, Mia. To keep you safe," Noah replied simply. "This world is dangerous, but with protection, you will be safe."

A new thought dawned on her. "Does that mean I have to be a soldier now?" The thought of wielding a weapon, of facing the horrors she'd witnessed, filled her with dread. Noah squeezed her hand gently. "No, Mia. You don't have to be a soldier. Lily, Elena, Riley, Reagan, and Emma, they fight because they choose to fight. David respects everyone's choice. You will be given the option, but you will never be forced." Mia chewed on her lip, considering this. The relief was palpable, but a sliver of uncertainty remained. She was used to being told what to do, her choices limited. This... this was new.

Chapter 33:

Old Ways, New World

The group fell into comfortable silence, the rhythmic crunch of their boots the only sound. The settlement came into view surprisingly quickly. The two men David had left behind were sitting on the porch, looking completely bewildered. As the war party approached, the two men scrambled to their feet, faces pale. "Afternoon, gentlemen," David greeted them with a deceptively gentle smile. "Finished cleaning up, I see." The larger man stammered, "Y-yes, sir. Just like you said. Buried them all proper."

David, standing before the two men he'd spared, and Jimmy, who looked like he might faint from sheer anxiety, radiated an unsettling calmness. Thomas stood silently beside him. "A community," David began, his voice carrying authority without being loud, "is like a body. Every part needs to work together, not against each other. If the hand steals from the mouth, the whole body suffers. You understand?" The larger of the two men, grunted an affirmative. The other, a wiry fellow, nodded nervously.

"You can't build a lasting community on fear and stolen resources," David continued, his gaze sweeping over them, "It will crumble from within. You need trust, cooperation, and shared goals. You need to produce, not just take." He gestured towards the surrounding fields, overgrown and neglected. "This land can feed you, clothe you, shelter you. But it takes work. It takes effort. And it takes everyone pulling in the same direction."

David outlined a plan to help the settlement become self-sufficient: seeds, tools, training. He spoke of irrigation, crop rotation, and defense against raiders. He even mentioned the possibility of bringing in some of Eli's farmhands to teach them about livestock. "We're not going to force you to become saints overnight," David said, a flicker of amusement in his eyes, "But we will hold you accountable. We'll be watching." He gestured to Jimmy. "Jimmy here is your governor."

The large man scoffed, a low rumble in his chest. "Jimmy? That weakling?" David's eyes narrowed, the mirth vanishing. "Jimmy understands the value of survival. He knows what it's like to be at the bottom, to be taken advantage of. And he's seen what happens when you fall back into your old ways. He's also seen exactly the lengths to which I will go to protect those who cannot protect themselves. Furthermore, just because Jimmy is in charge of these outer properties, doesn't mean he has to be the strongest. He just has to see the bigger picture."

David pointed toward the other settlement. "Jimmy already has good rapport with the people left at the other settlement, and he has favor with Eli." David gestured around the property. "You're going to be shorthanded for a while, so we'll help you as we go." He held up a finger. "However, if this community isn't worth the investment, I'll finish what I started."

Mia, tucked safely behind Noah, observed David with cautious curiosity. He was a puzzle, this man. He wielded life and death with equal ease yet spoke of eradication and cooperation with the same casual intensity. He was a benevolent dictator, a compassionate overlord, a walking contradiction wrapped in tactical gear. He wasn't what she expected from a leader who could cause so much death in a matter of minutes.

David signaled to the others, and everyone turned to leave. Thomas walked closely alongside David, while Seth and Elena brought up the rear. Mia and Noah followed along silently, close to each other. As they walked away from the settlement and toward their vehicles, Mia tugged at Noah's sleeve, her brow furrowed with concern. "Noah," she whispered, "Is David your father?"

Noah blinked, his usually impassive face betraying a hint of surprise. "No, Mia. David is not my father." Mia pondered this, her dark eyes fixed on David's retreating figure. Then her gaze shifted to Elena, who was laughing at something Seth had said. A thought came to Mia, as she noticed Elena's stunning appearance. "Elena is very pretty," she blurted out.

Noah nodded in agreement. "Yes, Mia. They are all pretty." Mia's brow furrowed again. Something about his response didn't sound quite right. "No, no," she corrected, "She's pretty." She was trying to point out that David had a very pretty wife, but Noah had said something that felt off. To Mia, it sounded like he was calling every woman in the group pretty. But maybe she was wrong.

As they reached the vehicles, Mia's eyes widened. Functioning vehicles! It was like stepping into a futuristic movie. The Ford Transit looked almost...normal, despite the dust and slight modifications. Noah helped her into the van, securing her next to him. Junior, Emma, and Riley were already inside, talking in low voices. Caleb, Marvin, Parker, and Scott clambered in after them.

The engine rumbled to life, a sound that Mia found surprisingly comforting. As the convoy rushed into motion, Mia's gaze swept over Emma and Riley. They were pretty, yes, but something else caught her attention: the slim, metal collars encircling their necks. They were solid, but ornate, almost like jewelry, but unsettling nonetheless. She leaned closer to Noah, then whispered. "What are those?"

"They are collars," Noah had begun, his Spanish halting but understandable. "Property collars, of Junior." The word "property" hung heavy in the air. Mia's widening eyes betrayed her unease. "Property?" she repeated, her voice barely a whisper. "Junior... is he their owner?" The implication was clear, and chilling.

Noah, usually so quiet and reserved, acknowledged grimly. "Yes. They are Junior's wives." He carefully omitted the explanation of the collars as symbols of submission. It was too nuanced, too layered with societal baggage to translate at this moment. He hoped she understood the basic premise: these women belonged to Junior.

Mia's gaze flicked back and forth between Emma and Riley. They didn't look like slaves. They didn't seem downtrodden or abused. In fact, they seemed...happy?

Confused, she turned back to Noah, her brow furrowed. "But... are they happy?"

Noah reached out and gently squeezed her leg, a gesture of reassurance. "Yes Mia. They love their husband very much, and he loves them. It's a symbol of their relationship. Do you understand?" A "a symbol of their relationship." The phrase tasted strange on her tongue. In her past, relationships were about power, about ownership in a far more brutal sense. This...this seemed different. Emma and Riley radiated a certain contentment, a quiet confidence that defied her expectations. If they were happy, truly happy... who was she to judge?

Then, the bombshell dropped. "Wait," she blurted, grabbing Noah's arm, her voice urgent. "One... or two?" She pointed at Emma, then at Riley, her confusion radiating like heat off the asphalt. Noah sighed internally. He'd anticipated this. "Three," he stated, enunciating slowly and clearly. "Junior has three wives. Emma, Riley, and Olivia." Mia's jaw hit the floor. A soft "Tres?" escaped her lips, laced with disbelief. It was a testament to her shock that she didn't even bother to phrase it as a question.

Before she could descend into total Spanish-infused meltdown, Noah calmly continued. "You'll see, Mia. When we get to the ranch. You'll see how it works. You'll see how Junior treats them. How they treat him." "But...how?" she sputtered, clearly struggling to reconcile this information with her worldview.

Noah shrugged, a hint of amusement flickering in his eyes. "You're used to seeing weak men, Mia. Selfish men.

Even lazy men. Men who take and take without giving anything in return. That's all you've ever known. So, I understand how difficult it is to understand this." He paused. He wanted her to see the difference, the potential for something better. "Everyone here... can see what you see, Mia. Everyone can see that Junior has three wives. They probably all thought the same thing.." He paused again, then dropped the next revelation. "Still, there is another woman on the ranch who is working very hard to become his fourth wife. Not to mention, his father, David, has nine."

The dust swirled around the convoy as David's convoy rolled to a stop in front of the sprawling ranch house. Mia, still reeling from the polygamous flash bang, clung to Noah's arm, her eyes wide. Thomas stood stiffly beside them, his own shock evident as he took in the sheer scale of the place. It was unlike anything he'd envisioned, far exceeding even Eli's fortified farm in both size and apparent prosperity. He noticed as Junior hopped out of the lead truck, Callie and Olivia ran to him and bear hugged him.

As predicted, the entire female population of the ranch seemed to materialize from thin air, rushing forward to greet their returning men. Mia's head swiveled, trying to keep up. Andrea embraced Scott with a relieved sigh, Jill threw her arms around Parker, Bonnie gave Seth a shy wave and then a beaming smile, Sophia practically leaped into Caleb's arms, and Sara engulfed Marvin in a tight hug. "Just breathe, Mia," Noah murmured, squeezing her hand again. "It's a lot, I know. But it will be over soon."

The sheer cleanliness of everything struck Mia next. At the settlement, dirt was a constant companion, clinging to everything, ingrained in their clothes and skin. Here, the ranch house gleamed white in the afternoon sun, the porch swept clean, flower boxes overflowing with vibrant blooms. It was like stepping into a different world, a world where beauty and order still existed. Thomas, too, seemed taken back. He'd expected a rough-and-tumble survivalist camp, not this...this oasis.

As they approached the house, Mia's eyes darted around, taking in the vastness of the place. The compound was huge! At the second settlement there was only one building, and the rest were crude shacks. Here in this area, there were gardens, a barn, even a work shed. It was a far cry from the squalor and unfair treatment she'd hardened at the hands of the men who occupied her old camp.

David noticed Mia's overwhelmed expression. He gently detached himself from Tiffany's embrace, a hug that looked less like a reassuring pat on the back, and more like dry humping, and stepped forward, a warm smile on his face. "Welcome to our home, Mia," he said, his voice kind and reassuring. "We're glad you're here. Don't worry, we'll give you time to adjust." He turned to Thomas, his gaze hardening slightly. "And you. You'll have a chance to prove yourself useful here. We believe in second chances, but don't mistake kindness for weakness."

Thomas swallowed hard, nodding dumbly. He could feel the weight of David's gaze, a gaze that seemed to pierce through him, assessing his every thought and intention.

Elena, who had been lingering near David, stepped forward, offering Mia a small smile. "Come on, Mia. Let's get you some water and something to eat. You must be exhausted." Mia followed, understanding the hospitality Noah spoke of.

As they walked toward the house, Mia's gaze drifted over those assembled. Then Jennifer locked onto Mia, and Mia also noticed Jennifer's necklace. Jennifer strode up to Mia, ignoring Noah. "Welcome to the family. I'm Jennifer, one of David's wives." She waved her hand as she gestured around her. "You can call me whatever you like, as long as it's respectful." Mia, stunned and dumbfounded, was at a loss. "Gracias."

Then as Mia turned, she noticed that many of the other women wore assorted necklaces and chokers, especially the group that gravitated toward David. She spotted Summer sporting a brilliant silver chain, Tiffany with a broad velvet band, and even Jessica, the smaller one, wore a black leather collar. It was... strange. Mia was dumbfounded at how brazen these women were. They all kissed David passionately, like his very presence was life-giving. She had never seen such open affection, especially not with so many people watching.

As they entered the house, Mia gasped. It was even more impressive inside. Sunlight streamed through the large, bullet-resistant French doors, illuminating the spotless living room. Kayla, meanwhile, had already anticipated their arrival. She ushered Mia toward a comfortable armchair, offering her a glass of cool water and a plate of sliced fruit. "Here," she said with a warm smile. "Eat something. You look like you haven't had a decent meal in days." Mia gratefully accepted the offering, taking a tentative bite of a juicy slice of watermelon. The sweetness exploded on her tongue, a taste she hadn't experienced in years. Tears welled up in her eyes. "It's okay," Kayla said softly, patting her hand. "You're home now. We'll take care of you."

Mia, still slightly overwhelmed, turned to Noah. "Is it normal? Or is it... a welcome celebration?" she asked. Noah, ever the stoic, gave a slight shrug. "Pretty normal," he replied, his gaze drifting toward the kitchen where Summer was now orchestrating what appeared to be a full-blown feast. "David's... got a thing for taking care of people." Mia blinked, processing this information. So, the lavish welcome wasn't just for her. This level of generosity, this... abundance, was simply part of their way of life. She was starting to suspect her concept of "normal" was about to undergo a radical overhaul.

Hesitantly, Mia spoke again. "Can...can I see the girl? Grace?" she asked, her voice laced with concern. She had heard whispers of a girl who had been hurt. Noah agreed. "Yeah. Grace is downstairs in the infirmary. Still recovering." He gestured for her to follow him. "Come on." Noah led Mia down a set of stairs, the air growing cooler with each step. The opulent atmosphere of the main house faded, replaced by the sterile scent of antiseptic and the soft hum of medical equipment. They entered a brightly lit room, the walls painted a calming pale green. It was small, but meticulously organized, clearly a space dedicated to healing.

And there she was. Grace. Lying peacefully in a hospital bed, hooked up to a monitor that beeped rhythmically, charting her vital signs. An IV drip infused blood slowly into her arm. Bandages swathed her chest, left side, and left arm, stark white against her pale skin.

Mia stopped just inside the doorway, her breath catching in her throat. The rumors hadn't prepared her for this. She had expected, perhaps, a fragile, weakened figure. But even in her injured state, Grace possessed an ethereal beauty. Her long lashes rested against her cheeks, her skin was smooth and porcelain-like, and the curve of her jaw was delicate and refined. She was like a sleeping angel, wounded but undeniably radiant.

Mia stared, mesmerized. So beautiful, she thought. So beautiful. Noah stood beside her, his usual stoicism softening slightly. "She's still pretty weak," he murmured, his voice unusually gentle. "The bullet... it did a lot of damage." Mia remained silent, unable to tear her gaze away from Grace. She felt a strange mix of emotions swirling within her: pity, admiration, and a touch of... envy? She quickly dismissed the thought. How could she be envious of someone so clearly suffering?

After what felt like an eternity, Mia finally found her voice. "She...she looks so young," she whispered, her Spanish accent thick. "She is young. Fifteen," Noah replied. "Just a girl." Fifteen. Mia was seventeen. Only two years separated them, yet Grace seemed worlds away, living in a world of hardship and responsibility Mia couldn't even fathom. "Will she be okay?" Mia asked, her voice tinged with anxiety. Noah hesitated. "She'll be okay. She's got David and his wives looking after her." He paused, a flicker of something unreadable in his eyes. "She'll get through it."

Mia chewed on her lip, her dark eyes filled with questions. "Does she have a boyfriend? A boy she likes?" Noah chuckled softly, shaking his head. "Yeah, she's got a guy. Probably got a bunch of them lined up if she wanted, but she only wants one. The only one she'll ever want. That guy next door, Kyle."

Mia's brow furrowed. "He's... special, then?" "Special? You could say that," Noah replied, leaning against the wall. "He's good with guns, and his sister is one of David's wives. But to Grace, he's everything. Her fiancé." Mia fell silent again, staring at Grace. Even in sleep, she seemed different. A strength radiated from her, despite her fragile state. "She's different." Noah straightened, his expression turning serious. "She is different, Mia. Grace has her father's strength, his knowledge. It's in her blood, just like Lily, just like Junior."

Mia tilted her head, confused. "It's... complicated," Noah said, waving off the question with his hand. "Don't worry about it. Just know she's tougher than she looks." A new wave of curiosity washed over Mia. "Can...can I meet him? Kyle?" Noah considered for a moment, then acknowledged. "He's resting in the next room. He got shot too. Andrea and Tiffany are keeping him sedated, something about making him heal faster. Okay, but don't wake him. He needs all the rest he can get."

As Noah and Mia turned to leave the room, the infirmary door swung open, and Andrea burst in, her face etched with concern. "Noah, there you are!" Andrea exclaimed, her eyes flickering between him and Mia. She stopped short, noticing Mia. "Oh, hello. I don't think we've met. I'm Andrea." Mia, momentarily tongue-tied, managed a small curtsy. "Hello, ma'am. I'm Mia."

"Mia," Noah said, stepping forward slightly. "Andrea is Scott's wife. She's our doctor. She's helping Grace and Kyle out." Andrea's brow furrowed slightly. "Noah, what's going on? You know David doesn't like loitering." "She was just… uh…" He floundered for a moment. "She was curious about Grace." Andrea's expression softened a fraction. "Ah, I see. Well, Mia, welcome to our…rather unconventional family. It's good to have another pair of hands, even if they're new to all this." She gestured around the room. "As you can see, we're a little worried at the moment. But perhaps later, when things have calmed down, we can get to know each other better."

"Wife?" Mia asked, her brow furrowing. "She's married to… Scott?" Her eyes widened, picturing the mocking, quiet man who had helped with the rescue only hours earlier. "The scout?" Noah, taken back by her immediate confusion, chuckled softly. "Yeah, Andrea is Scott's wife. Pretty cool, right? They're a good team." He leaned in slightly, lowering his voice. "And Scott's more than just a scout, you know. He's our butcher too. Volunteered for the job." He paused, remembering something else. "Oh, and their son, Mike? He's the kid who gave Grace CPR after… well, you know."

Mia's mouth formed a silent 'o'. The pieces were starting to fit together, but the sheer interconnectedness of this strange community was overwhelming. "So everyone knows everyone?" she asks, already knowing the answer. "Ah," Mia said softly, processing the information. The idea of Scott, the quiet, capable scout, teasing David, the enigmatic patriarch, was both amusing and intriguing. But as she looked at Noah, a different kind of curiosity sparked in her eyes. "Noah?" she hesitated, "Can I see your room?"

Noah blinked, surprised by the sudden shift in topic. He hadn't expected her to ask to see his room. He scratched the back of his neck, considering the request. It wasn't an unreasonable one, he supposed. She was new, needed to acclimate, and seeing her room might help her feel more comfortable. He didn't see any harm in it.

"Sure, Mia. Come on." He gestured towards the door leading out into the garage. "It's not much, but it's mine." He reached the far end of the hallway, stopping at the first door on the left. "Here it is," Noah said simply, reaching for the handle. He pushed the door open, stepping aside to let Mia enter first.

The room was small, functional, and undeniably masculine. The queen bed was neatly made, covered with a simple dark blue comforter. A small wooden desk stood against one wall, cluttered with various items. As Noah stepped inside, he reached back and hung his rifle on the holder that was mounted next to the door. With his back still turned towards Mia, he said, "Like I said, it's not much, but it's mine. I don't spend a lot of time here."

The words were barely out of his mouth when he felt her presence behind him. He sensed a shift in the air, a change in the atmosphere that he couldn't quite explain. Then, he heard the soft touch of fabric falling to the floor. Noah froze. What was happening? He hadn't expected this. He slowly turned around, his eyes widening in surprise and confusion.

Mia stood before him, her dark eyes filled with a mixture of nervousness and determination. She had already removed her clothes. "Mia?" he asked. She stepped closer, her gaze fixed on his. "Am I not your wife?" Noah swallowed hard. He understood what she was saying, what she thought she was supposed to do. "Mia, wait," he said gently, reaching out a hand to stop her. "It doesn't have to be like this."

Noah stared at Mia, her nakedness, a clash of cultures and desires. He hadn't anticipated her unwavering conviction in fulfilling what she believed to be her marital duty. "Mia," he repeated, his voice a little stronger this time, laced with a gentle plea. "It's not like that here. You don't owe me anything. I want you to be comfortable, to be happy. We don't have to do this if you don't want to." He gestured towards the pile of clothes on the floor. "Please, get dressed. We can talk about this."

Mia's dark eyes searched his, confusion warring with a deep-seated conviction. "Why not?" she asked, her voice trembling slightly. "I am your wife. It is my duty." He understood the words, it was her duty as his wife, the sentiment behind them. He understood the weight of tradition that pressed upon her, the expectations she carried. He just didn't know how to dismantle them, how to explain that here, in this strange new world they were building, things could be different.

"Because," Noah began, running a hand over his head, "I want you to want me, Mia. Not because you feel you have to. I don't want you doing something out of obligation." He took a step closer, his voice softening. "I want you to desire me." The words felt clumsy, inadequate, but they were the truth. He wanted her to see him, to choose him, not to simply fulfill a role she'd been taught to play.

Mia's expression hardened, a flicker of something akin to anger flashing in her eyes. She shook her head, her long, dark hair swaying around her shoulders. "I don't understand," she said, her voice firm. "A marriage is work. Sometimes you don't like the work, but you do it. Even wives can hate their husbands, but they still work on their marriage."

Noah sighed. He was losing her. He could see the frustration building in her, the sense that he was rejecting not just her advances, but everything she believed about marriage, about her role as a wife. He felt a pang of guilt, realizing the enormity of what he was asking of her, of the cultural chasm he was trying to bridge with just a few words. "Okay," he said, trying a different approach. "Okay, let's talk about it. But please, Mia, put your clothes on. You must be cold."

But Mia stood her ground, her arms crossed defiantly. "No," she declared, her voice rising. "I won't dress. I won't eat. I won't do anything until you are my husband." Noah stared at her, dumbfounded. This was escalating quickly. He could see the stubborn set of her jaw, the determination in her eyes. He knew he couldn't force her to do anything, but he also couldn't let her go hungry or remain naked in his room. He had to find a way to reach her, to make her understand.

He lowered his voice, trying to project calm and reason. "Mia, you're being unreasonable. You can't just refuse to eat. It's not healthy. And you'll catch a cold." "Then be my husband," she retorted, her voice laced with impatience. "If you do not consummate our marriage, our union will be annulled. And I should just go back to the settlement!"

The last sentence hit him like a punch to the gut. Annulled? Go back to the settlement? The thought was horrifying. He couldn't let that happen. He'd rescued her from a life of servitude and potential abuse. He couldn't, wouldn't, allow her to return to that hellhole. Noah ran his hand over his head again, his mind racing. David had told him that Mia had to be taken care of. David had suggested Noah.

He had to turn to David for help. "Okay, Mia, stay here." Noah turned to leave. "Where are you going?" Mia demanded. "I have to go get someone," Noah replied. "I will be right back." He left the room and ran to find David. He found David in the main living room, surrounded by a chaotic scene of domesticity. The air was thick with the sounds of conversation, laughter, and the general cacophony of a large, unconventional family.

Noah approached David, his face a mask of despair. "David, I need your help," he blurred out, interrupting the lively scene. David turned, his intelligent eyes immediately registering Noah's distress. He raised an eyebrow, a hint of amusement flickering across his face. "Having some marital difficulties, Noah?" "It's...complicated," Noah admitted, his cheeks flushing slightly. "Mia...she's not understanding. She thinks I'm disrespecting her by not...you know..."

David chuckled, a low rumble in his chest. "Ah, the clash of cultures. I anticipated this might be a challenge. Come, let's talk." He gestured for Noah to follow him to a quieter corner of the room, away from the prying eyes and ears of the rest of the family. "She won't get dressed, and she refuses to eat until I, in her words, 'be her husband.' And if I don't, she said our marriage will be annulled and she'll go back to the settlement. David, I can't let that happen." Noah's voice was strained with anxiety.

David listened patiently, his expression thoughtful. "I see," he said finally. "This is a delicate situation. Mia is acting out of deeply ingrained beliefs and a genuine fear of abandonment. To her, consummating the marriage is not just a physical act, it's a symbol of commitment and acceptance." He paused, stroking his chin. "Tell me, Noah, if you wanted a Latina wife, why are you treating Mia like a white girl?" Noah gasped. "What do you mean?" Noah asked, genuinely confused. "I'm trying to be respectful. I thought pressing her would be wrong. I figured maybe, if we took it slow, she'd feel more comfortable. I thought that was what you were implying I do when you rescued her!"

David sighed, the amusement gone from his face, replaced by a grandfatherly concern. "Noah, my boy, you're thinking with your 21st-century brain, and that's admirable, but it's missing the mark entirely. You rescued her, yes, but you didn't rescue her to turn her into someone else. You wanted a Latina wife, steeped in tradition. That tradition, for

164

Mia, demands certain... assurances. You're inadvertently insulting her by holding back. You're making her feel like she's not good enough, that you find her unattractive, or that you regret the rescue."

Noah's eyes widened. "I...I never thought of it that way. But she seems so...scared." "Scared, yes, but is she acting out of fear, or obligation?" David leaned closer, lowering his voice. "Think, Noah. If Mia felt obligated, coerced into this marriage, she would have refused you immediately. She would have clung to Isabella, pleaded to be taken back. Did she do that?"

Noah shook his head slowly. "No. She was quiet, but she seemed...resigned, maybe? Accepting." "Exactly." David snapped his fingers. "Resignation is not the same as reluctance. Of course she's afraid, but not regretful. She's testing you, Noah. She's trying to figure out if you're truly committed, if you truly desire her, not just a compliant housekeeper who speaks Spanish."

Noah ran a hand over his head, his brow furrowed. "So... she wants me to...?" He trailed off, unable to articulate the question fully. David chuckled softly, clapping Noah on the shoulder. "Let's just say that a little old-fashioned courtship might be in order. Show her you value her traditions. Speak to her in Spanish. Compliment her cooking, even if it's just the smell of it. Let her know you see her, not just as a rescue, but as a woman, a beautiful woman, that you desire."

Noah swallowed hard. "But what if I'm wrong? What if I move too fast and scare her away?" "You won't," David said with unwavering confidence. "I know Mia. She's testing you, yes, but she's also drawn to you. She saw you, Noah. She saw your kindness, your quiet strength, and your respect, even if that respect is currently misdirected. She wouldn't have accepted the marriage if there wasn't something there."

Noah looked down at his boots. "Okay…okay, I think I understand. But… what should I do? Right now? She won't even come out of the room unless I promise to… well, you know." David's eyes twinkled. "First, tell me, Noah. Do you like her? Are you attracted to her?" Noah's head shot up, his cheeks flushing a deeper shade of red. "Of course I do! She's beautiful, David. I wouldn't have asked for a Latina wife if I didn't value that." He paused, a flicker of vulnerability in his eyes. "I just… I didn't want to mess it up."

David nodded, a smile playing on his lips. "Good. Honesty is key. Now, here's what you're going to do. Go to your room. Speak to her in Spanish. Tell her you understand that you have been insensitive to her traditions, and that you are sorry. Tell her that you find her incredibly beautiful and that you are honored to be her husband. Then, tell her that you desire her, but that you also want to respect her wishes and pace. And then…," David paused for dramatic effect, "Then give her what she wants. In fact, I don't want to even see her walking around the ranch tomorrow without some sort of shake in her legs."

Chapter 34:

The Language of Skin

Noah stood frozen in the doorway, the weight of David's...advice settling heavily on his shoulders. He'd expected a lecture, maybe a gentle chiding about patience. He definitely hadn't anticipated a direct order to, well, fulfill his matrimonial duties with such...enthusiasm.

Taking another deep breath, he steeled himself and pushed the door open. The sight that greeted him almost sent him stumbling back out. Mia was indeed still naked, but the drama had apparently subsided, replaced by curiosity. She was gazing intently at the LCD window in his room, her dark eyes wide as she examined the different scenes displayed on the screen. He had to admit, she looked...amazing.

Then she turned, her earlier frustration etched back onto her face. The image was slightly less amazing. Before he could launch into his carefully rehearsed apology, he blurred out the first thing that came to mind. "Shower first." The words hung in the air, sounding incredibly lacking even to his own ears. He braced himself for another wave of Spanish-infused indignation. Instead, Mia's expression softened, a hint of a smile playing on her lips. "Shower?" she repeated, tilting her head. "Yes. We've been outside in the heat all day."

Relief washed over Noah. He hadn't completely ruined everything. Yet. A bright smile spread across Mia's face, chasing away the last vestiges of her frustration.

Snatching his hand, she tugged him towards the small bathroom. "Together," she chirped, her eyes sparkling with playful anticipation. Noah's carefully crafted speech vanished from his mind, replaced by a surge of...panic. This was happening. Now. He swallowed hard, trying to ignore the conflicting emotions warring within him. He wanted to do this right, to be respectful, to build a real connection. But David's... encouragement to satisfy her, also echoed in his mind.

Noah stood frozen in the doorway of the small bathroom. He hadn't anticipated this level of enthusiasm. He had expected tears, maybe a silent, resentful compliance. He certainly hadn't envisioned a cheerful invitation to a shared shower. Maybe David's assertion that he needed to pleasure her was right. He really had to shake off his Tennessee boy ideas of courtship

Mia, oblivious to his inner turmoil, was already fiddling with the shower controls, her brow furrowed in concentration. She tentatively turned a knob, then yelped as a burst of cold water sprayed her bare feet. Noah winced. "Easy there," he said, stepping closer. "Let me show you." He adjusted the temperature, finding the sweet spot between scalding and freezing. A plume of steam began to rise, filling the small space with a comforting warmth.

Mia giggled, her earlier reservations seemingly forgotten. "Hot water!" she exclaimed, testing the water with her hand. "I haven't felt this in so long!" A pang of guilt shot through Noah. He couldn't imagine going without a hot shower for so long. The thought of what Mia had endured, the hardship and lack of basic necessities, made him even more determined to make this work.

Noah cleared his throat. "How long can we shower?" Mia asked, her question laced with a hint of anxiety. Noah blinked, momentarily confused. "As long as you want," he replied, trying to sound casual. "We have unlimited clean and hot water. David made sure of it." Mia's jaw dropped. "Unlimited!" she breathed, her eyes wide with disbelief. "Are you serious?" "Really," Noah confirmed with a smile. He grabbed a fluffy towel from the rack and a clean t-shirt from his meager wardrobe, setting them on the counter. "Here, you'll need these later."

She clutched the wash rag to her chest, her eyes gleaming with gratitude. Then, without warning, she reached out, grabbing his hand once more. "Come," she insisted, tugging him towards the bathtub. "Together." Noah's eyes widened. "Together?" He stammered slightly, stepping back to pace. "Mia, I… I appreciate the enthusiasm, but I think… maybe for the first shower, you should just… you know, relax and enjoy the water. By yourself."

Mia's expression hardened slightly. She tilted her head, studying him with an intensity that made him squirm. "You don't like me?" she asked, her voice soft, but loaded with enough dramatic weight to sink a battleship. "A good husband shows his love. My abuela always said, 'A cold husband brings cold home.'"

Noah groaned inwardly. Abuela. Of course, there was an Abuela. He sighed, surrendering to the inevitable. "Alright, alright. Together. Together, it is." He started unbuttoning his shirt, trying to project an air of casual enjoyment that he definitely didn't feel. He managed to shuck off his shirt and jeans, leaving him in his boxers. Mia clapped her hands. "Yes! Now we're getting somewhere!" She gestured impatiently at his lower half. "But... these must go too."

Noah swallowed hard. "Mia," he said slowly, "are you sure? I mean, we just met today... I don't want you to feel pressured or uncomfortable." He knew he sounded like a complete idiot. Mia rolled her eyes, a gesture that somehow managed to convey both amusement and exasperation. "Pressure? Take them off or I'll tear them off myself!" She punctuated her statement with a playful yank, pulling him closer to the shower.

Noah's eyes widened in alarm. "Okay, okay! No need for violence!" He quickly shed his boxers, trying to avoid eye contact with Mia, who now stood with her arms crossed watching him with a critical eye. He stepped into the shower stall, turning his back to her as he turned on the water on the opposite side. The water cascaded over him, warm and surprisingly soothing. He heard Mia gasp as he joined her, the small space suddenly feeling minuscule.

"Oh, my God!" Mia exclaimed, her voice echoing off the tile. "Two!" Noah blinked, turning to see Mia pointing, wide-eyed, at the two shower heads, one on each side of the stall. "Two?" he repeated, confused. "Two shower heads!" she repeated, her eyes wide and dancing with excitement. "How naughty!"

Noah chuckled, the tension finally starting to ease. "Oh, yeah. David installed those. Practicality, I guess. You can get all the bits clean." Mia blinked, tilting her head. "Practical? No, I don't think so. I think David knew exactly what he was doing. Even the bedrooms have queen beds. Besides, David has nine wives. David encourages love."

Noah relented, a sheepish grin spreading across his face. He couldn't argue with her logic, especially not when delivered with such playful conviction. David, the benevolent, if slightly eccentric, patriarch of their little community, was indeed a master strategist, even when it came to matters of the heart... and shower fixtures. He soaped Mia's back, and she returned the favor. Noah giggled, telling her he needed to learn better Spanish so he could understand her sense of humor.

The shower lasted a long time. The two shower heads proved to be as efficient as David had likely intended, washing away not only the grime of the day but also a good deal of Noah's anxiety. Mia, with her infectious energy and surprising forwardness, managed to coax him out of his shell, making him laugh more in the past hour than he had in weeks.

Finally, they emerged from the steaming stall, both flushed and slightly giddy. Mia grabbed a towel and vigorously dried herself off, humming a lively tune under her breath. Noah, still a little dazed, followed suit, trying to ignore the lingering scent of soap and the pleasant warmth spreading through his veins.

Mia, now dry and radiating an almost ethereal glow, plopped down on Noah's bed, completely calm. Noah averted his gaze, his cheeks burning again. He shuffled towards his dresser, intending to grab a pair of boxers and a t-shirt, anything to break the awkward silence and give him a semblance of composure. "Noah," Mia said, her voice soft but firm. He stopped in his tracks, his back still to her. "Yeah?" "Come." He hesitated. "I... I just need to get dressed." Mia giggled, a sound that was both innocent and undeniably alluring. "Why? Don't be shy."

Noah took a deep breath and turned around. Mia was sitting cross-legged on the bed, her dark eyes sparkling with mischief. She beckoned him with a slender finger. His every instinct screamed at him to either run or... well, not run. He stood there, frozen, a battle raging within him. On one side was his ingrained sense of propriety, his awkwardness, and the overwhelming feeling of being out of his depth. On the other side was Mia, beautiful, vivacious, and seemingly unfazed by the whirlwind of events that had led them to this moment.

"Mia," he started, his voice a croak. "I... I don't know what to do." Mia's playful expression softened, her eyes filled with a surprising vulnerability. She rose from the bed, her movement graceful and fluid, and approached Noah cautiously. The small space seemed to shrink with every step she took, the silence amplifying the nervous flutter in Noah's chest.

She stopped a few feet away, tilting her head, her gaze searching his face. "Me neither," she confessed, her voice barely a whisper. Noah frowned, surprised. "You...you don't?" Mia shook her head, her dark hair swaying gently. She took another step closer, her voice gaining a little strength. "I'm a virgin, Noah. I've never kissed anyone." The confession hung in the air, thick with unspoken emotion. Noah's eyes widened. He knew she was young, but the full weight of her innocence struck him. The image of her, enslaved, flashed through his mind, fueling a surge of protective anger.

"And... luckily, they rescued us before someone bought me." Her voice trembled slightly on the last word, hinting at the terror she had faced. Noah's heart ached. He reached out, his hand hovering near her arm, unsure if he should touch her. "Mia..." She looked up at him, her eyes shimmering with a mixture of fear and determination. "I want to be a woman, Noah. With you. Here. Now."

The bluntness of her statement, spoken with such raw honesty, took his breath away. All the carefully constructed walls he had built around his emotions crumbled. This wasn't just about him anymore. It was about her, about giving her the agency that had been nearly stolen from her, about showing her kindness and respect in a world that had offered her neither.

He lowered his hand, his gaze fixed on hers. "Are... are you sure, Mia?" "Yes," she replied, her voice unwavering. "I'm sure. But... I'm scared." Noah finally allowed himself to touch her, gently taking her hand in his. Her skin was soft and warm, her fingers trembling slightly. He looked into her eyes, searching for any sign of doubt, any hint of coercion. He saw only vulnerability and a brave, unwavering trust.

A wave of tenderness washed over him. He wouldn't rush her. He wouldn't pressure her. He would be gentle, patient, and above all, respectful. He would show her that intimacy could be about more than just physical pleasure, that it could be about connection, about trust, about love. "Okay," he said softly, squeezing his hand. "Okay. We'll take it slow. We don't have to do anything you don't want to do."

He led her over to the bed, sitting down beside her. The small space suddenly felt less daunting, filled with a shared understanding and a growing sense of connection. "Tell me what you're afraid of," he encouraged, his voice gentle. "Anything. No matter how silly it sounds." Mia hesitated, then took a deep breath. "I don't know how it'll feel. Isabella...she didn't tell me much. Just that it's...important." Noah smiled slightly. "It is important. But it's also… it can be beautiful, Mia. It can be about sharing something special with someone you care about."

She leaned forward, her movements tentative. Then, she did something unexpected. She kissed him. It was a shy, hesitant kiss at first, her lips barely brushing against his. Noah remained still, allowing her to set the pace. He wanted her to feel in control, to understand that she was the one calling the shots. He closed his eyes, savoring the innocent sweetness of the moment.

Then, something shifted. The kiss deepened. Mia's grip on his hand tightened, her body pressing closer to his. The initial tentativeness melted away, replaced by a burgeoning passion that surprised them both. Noah responded in kind, his own desires awakening. He cupped her face in his hands, deepening the kiss, his tongue gently exploring her mouth.

He felt her shiver, a small tremor that ran through her entire body. He pulled back slightly, his eyes searching hers. He needed to make sure she was still comfortable, still willing. She nodded, her eyes wide and luminous. The fear was still there, but it was mingled with a newfound excitement, a sense of anticipation. He saw a trust in her gaze that humbled him.

He moved his lips to her neck, planting soft kisses along her collarbone. He felt her pulse quicken beneath his touch. He could smell the sweet scent of her hair, the clean, floral fragrance of the soap they had used in the shower. Instinctively, his kisses moved lower, tracing a path down her chest, over her ribs, his lips lingering on the curve of her stomach. He reveled in the feel of her skin beneath his lips, the soft, delicate texture that felt so foreign and yet so right. He didn't know why she tasted so good, but every kiss, every lick, every gentle nibble was like a flame on Mia's skin. He traced the line of her hip with his tongue, a low groan escaping his lips. He felt her hands clutch at his head, pulling him closer.

Mia was writhing on his bed, as if every kiss was shooting up her spine and exploding, like sparks in her head. She gasped, her breath coming in short, shallow bursts. She had never felt anything like this before, this swirling vortex of pleasure and sensation. Fear was still present, but it was fading, being replaced by a dizzying excitement, a sense of abandon she had never known she possessed. She felt completely exposed, completely vulnerable, but also strangely powerful. She was in control, she was choosing this, she was allowing herself to experience this.

Noah continued his exploration, his touch becoming more confident, more intimate. He knew he was walking a fine line, pushing her boundaries but not crossing them. He was constantly monitoring her reactions, watching her face for any sign of discomfort or distress. He reached a hand down, gently caressing her thigh. She flinched slightly, but didn't pull away. He paused, giving her a chance to object. She didn't.

He repeated the motion, his fingers slowly moving higher, tracing the inside of her leg. She gasped again, her body arching towards him. He felt a tremor run through her, a sign of her growing arousal. He reached between her legs, his fingers gently exploring the sensitive flesh. Mia cried out, a small, involuntary sound that filled the room. He paused, his breath catching in his throat. He was so close, he could feel her trembling, her desire radiating towards him.

He looked up at her, his eyes questioning. "Are you sure, Mia? We can stop. We can stop right now if you want to." She looked back at him, her eyes filled with a mixture of fear and longing. She hesitated for a moment, then agreed. "Yes. Don't stop." Now, she laid on his bed, naked and exposed, her heart pounding against her ribs like a trapped bird.

Noah leaned down, brushing his beard against her cheek. He kissed her softly, a gentle exploration that sent shivers down her spine. Then, he moved lower, his lips tracing a path down her neck, across her collarbone. Mia gasped, her fingers clutching at the sheets. She understood the mechanics of sex, the biological imperative, but this...

this was something entirely different. This was intimacy, a merging of souls that felt both terrifying and exhilarating.

He continued his descent, his breath warm against her skin. He paused at her stomach, pressing a soft kiss there before moving lower still. Mia's breath hitched. She knew, intellectually, what was coming, but the reality of it, the sheer audacity of his intent, felt a wave of panic surging through her. This was forbidden, taboo, something whispered about in hushed tones among the women of her village.

Yet, she couldn't bring herself to stop him. A strange, insistent curiosity had taken root within her, a desire to experience everything, to feel everything. She squeezed her eyes shut, bracing herself for the unknown. Then, his lips touched her. A strangled cry escaped her lips, a sound of pure, unadulterated shock. It was nothing like she had imagined. There was no pain, only a dizzying sensation, a wave of heat that washed over her, leaving her breathless and disoriented. She writhed beneath him, her hips instinctively arching towards his mouth.

He tasted her, her sweat and desire, and the intensity of it was overwhelming. She had never felt so vulnerable, so exposed, yet also so incredibly alive. She was a whirlwind of sensation, a storm of pleasure and confusion. Noah was careful, his movements gentle and deliberate. He watched her face, gauging her reactions, wanting to ensure that she was enjoying this, that she wasn't overwhelmed. He knew this was new for her, a landscape unknown. He wanted to be her guide, her patient and understanding lover.

He heard her soft whimpers, felt her body trembling beneath him. He knew she was close, on the precipice of something profound. He increased his pace, his tongue and lips working magic, building the tension, drawing her closer and closer to the edge. Mia's world dissolved, the room fading away, replaced by a kaleidoscope of colors and sensations. She cried out again, a long, drawn-out moan that echoed in the silence. Her body convulsed, her muscles clenching and releasing in a series of involuntary spasms. She was floating, weightless, adrift in a sea of pillows.

And then, it crested. A wave of intense, overwhelming ecstasy washed over her, leaving her gasping and breathless. She clung to Noah, her nails digging into his back, her body shaking with the force of the orgasm. Slowly, the intensity subsided, the colors faded, and the world began to come back into focus. She laid there, spent and exhausted, her body still tingling with aftershocks.

Noah raised his head, his eyes filled with concern. "Mia? Are you alright?" She nodded, unable to speak. She felt raw, exposed, like she had been turned inside out. But beneath the vulnerability, she felt something else, something new and powerful. She felt alive. He kissed her forehead, his touch gentle and reassuring. "You taste amazing," he whispered. She finally found her voice, her words a breathless murmur. "I...I don't understand. What was that?" He smiled, a knowing smile that crinkled the corners of his eyes. "That, my love, was just the beginning."

Inside the cavernous Smithy, however, a small measure of relief could be found. The earth-sheltered structure trapped the cool air, offering a welcome respite from the brutal heat outside. Tiffany, clad in her usual jeans and button up shirt, knelt beside the large sow, gently stroking its bristly back. The seven piglets, a wriggling mass of pink and snorts, jostled for position around their mother. She glanced up at Thomas, his young face etched with curiosity, and smiled. "Aren't they something?" she said, her voice warm and inviting. Thomas stood awkwardly, his eyes darting around the space. He seemed ill at ease, a fish out of water in this strange, cooperative environment.

"Why aren't they in the barn?" he finally asked, his voice hesitant. Tiffany chuckled, a sound that filled the Smithy with unexpected cheer. "Good question, Thomas. We're using the Smithy for quarantine right now. We need to make sure these little guys are healthy before we introduce them to the rest of the herd. Don't want to risk spreading any diseases."

Josh, looking surprisingly comfortable in his blue work overalls, his strong hands gently guiding a piglet back to its mother's teat. "Yeah, we plan on building a dedicated pig enclosure onto the barn later. But for now, this is the pig penthouse." He nodded slowly, taking in the scene. He'd expected… something different. He expected to be put to work constantly, to be shouted at. Instead, he was watching a woman tend to pigs, and a hardened security guy acting as a gentle, if somewhat sarcastic, midwife.

"It's a lot of work, isn't it?" he ventured, thinking of the effort it must take to care for so many animals, to maintain the ranch, to keep everything running. Josh straightened up, wiping his brow with the back of his hand. "It is," he agreed. "But the thing is, everyone contributes. It's not like one person is stuck doing everything. We all pitch in, help each other out." He gestured around the Smithy. "Tiffany is the expert on the animals here. However, everyone helps her out, even David. Because everyone contributes, the workload is spread out. It's easier than if it all piled up on one person."

Thomas was silent for a moment, processing this information. In Eli's community, work was doled out unevenly, with the strong taking advantage of the weak. There was little sense of shared responsibility, and even less of camaraderie. Seeing Josh, normally a picture of tactical readiness, tending to piglets was particularly jarring. He'd always pictured him as a stern enforcer, not a... farmer.

"You look...comfortable," Thomas said, a hint of surprise in his voice. Josh laughed, a deep, genuine sound. "I am. Grew up on a farm, you know? The tactical stuff came later, after I met Lily." He grinned, a flash of white teeth against his tanned face. "But this is where I'm most at home. Out here, working with the land, with the animals. It's in my blood." Tiffany, who had been cleaning a particularly stubborn piglet, who was now squealing his displeasure, nodded in agreement without looking up. "Josh is a natural. Animals respond to him. Plus, he's handy to have around when things break." She turned her attention back to the sow, gently palpating its belly. "We don't actually need the animals to survive, we have plenty of food. However, it's going to get rough out there and lots of animals won't survive. So we're building our herds now, improving the breed lines."

Suddenly, a wave of anxiety washed over Thomas. All of this... this community, this shared responsibility, these people who seemed to genuinely care for each other... it was so different from what he knew. He swallowed hard, the words catching in his throat. "Are... are people going to hate me here?" he blurted out, the question hanging in the humid air. "Because of what I did?" He couldn't even bring himself to say Grace's name aloud. The memory of her falling to the ground, Kyle's anguished yell, it all played on repeat in his mind.

Tiffany finally looked up, her expression unreadable. She wiped her hands on a rag, a slow, deliberate movement. "Probably," she said bluntly. "There are probably still people here who want you dead. You put a bullet into a fifteen-year-old girl." Thomas flinched, the words hitting him like a physical blow. "But," Tiffany continued, her voice softening slightly, "David already made the decision to give you a second chance. And nobody disobeys David. So you're here. Now, what you do with that second chance is up to you." She leveled a direct gaze at him, her eyes hard but not unkind. "Just don't expect anyone to forget what happened overnight. It will take time, and a lot of work. You have to earn their trust."

"I... I understand," Thomas mumbled. "I just... I wanted to help Eli. I saw her setting the trap, I knew she was strong." He took a deep breath. "I didn't know that guy was her boyfriend. She just seemed... too young. I wanted to give her an opportunity. I thought I was saving her." He finally managed to ask. "What does she do here? For the ranch?"

Josh looked over to Tiffany, before turning back to Thomas. He scratched his chin, a thoughtful frown on his face. "Well, son," he drawled, his voice laced with a hint of his country upbringing, "Grace ain't just some girl, and Kyle ain't just some fella. They're more important than you realize." Tiffany nodded in agreement. Lowering her voice, she said, "Grace teaches all the kids here. Everything from math and history to language. She's a natural with them, patient and kind." She paused. "She also teaches hand-to-hand combat, movement, and music.

Thomas' eyebrows shot up. "Combat? But she's..." Josh chuckled. "Sweet as pie, ain't she? Don't let that fool you. That girl's tougher than a two-dollar steak. She's also our infiltrator. She's got a knack for getting places most can't, seeing things others miss. Grace is a trapper, a tracker, a scout and a good cook. She can read the land like a book. And can bake a pie that'll make you wanna slap your mama." "Not to mention." Tiffany added. "Her and Lily make our body armor. Particularly for the women. It's a whole process."

"You know, Thomas," Tiffany said, her voice soft and reassuring. "We're not here to punish you. We're here to help you understand why what you did was wrong. And we're here to help you learn how to be part of a community." Thomas chewed on his lip, his eyes wide with a new mixture of fear and apprehension. "So... so you think Grace will, like, kill me?"

Josh barked out a laugh, slapping his knee. "Nah, son. Grace ain't the type to hold a grudge. She's got too much good in her for that. Besides," he smiled, "she's the victim here. She'll probably forgive you before she recovers. That's just the kind of gal she is. Now, Kyle, on the other hand..." He let the sentence hang in the air, his grin fading slightly. Tiffany nodded grimly.

"Kyle," she echoed, "is a different story. He nearly watched his fiancé die. He held her in his arms, bleeding. He saw the life almost drain out of her. He's got every right to be furious." Josh leaned forward, his voice dropping to a near whisper. "And don't forget about David. You shot his daughter. You think that would have gone over easy? The man rewrites history for fun, and you popped a cap in his little girl. You messed with his family, son. That's a big mistake."

Thomas's face paled further. "David? He seems... nice. He's been explaining things and hasn't yelled or anything." Tiffany chuckled, a low, throaty sound that didn't quite reach her eyes. "David is nice, Thomas. He's also the most dangerous man any of us have ever met. He's got a patience that could wear down mountains, and a resolve that's unshakeable. He's also fiercely protective of his family. And, let's be honest, he would have killed you in a heartbeat."

Josh nodded. "David also sees potential in everyone. Even you, apparently. That's why you're here, getting the 'understanding and community' treatment, and not hanging from the nearest oak tree." Tiffany sighed, running a hand through her hair. "Honestly, Thomas, I hope Grace recovers fully, and soon. For your sake, more than hers."

Meanwhile, in Noah's room, a different kind of lesson was underway. The small space was filled with the sounds of labored breathing and unrestrained joy. Mia, still naked, surrounded Noah with the fervor of a woman possessed. She had found a new world of sensation, and she was determined to explore every inch of it. "Faster, mi amor! Faster!" Mia urged, her voice a breathless plea. Noah, Astride the bed with her, grunted in response, his hands gripping her hips as he matched her fervent rhythm. The image on the screen blurred in their peripheral vision, the vendors' cries momentarily fading under Mia's escalating fervor.

Suddenly, Mia threw her head back, a guttural cry escaping her lips. The moment of climax hit her with a visible force, her body arching as she squeezed her eyes shut. When it subsided, she looked towards the LCD screen with almost a crazed grin. "Look at me, this little girl is fucking a big, strong gringo! I'm a chingona now! I let him lick me! I sucked his cock! I'm going to be my husband's puta!" she declared to the digital marketplace, her voice echoing with both triumph and unabashed desire.

Noah, still trying to catch his breath, could only manage a choked laugh. "Mia, my God, you're something else," he said, his voice thick with affection. But Mia wasn't done. As the aftershocks of her orgasm rippled through her, a gleam entered her eyes. "Now, mi amor! It's time for my favorite part!" she announced, shifting her weight so she was kneeling over him. Noah, despite his slight bewilderment, couldn't help but be intrigued. "Your favorite part? And what might that be?" he asked, a hint of anticipation in his voice.

Mia's answer was immediate. With a mischievous laugh, she proceeded to gather her cum from between her legs, smearing it across his chest in broad strokes. "My canvas!

184

I'm going to paint you like an Aztec warrior!" she exclaimed, giggling as she worked. Noah, despite the initial surprise, found himself enjoying the sensation. It was... different. He couldn't deny the primal thrill of her actions, the way her touch sent shivers down his spine. "You know," he said, a playful smile spreading across his face, "I think I prefer this to finger painting." Mia snorted, tilting her head to examine her handiwork. "You need more! More art!" she declared, before leaning down to capture more, this time spreading it across his cheek with a theatrical flourish.

Chapter 35:

The Seed of Sanctuary

Down in the maintenance bunker, within the hydroponics greenhouse, Brian hummed along to an anime song as he meticulously pruned a row of tomato plants. Seo-Yeon, her pregnant belly a prominent globe, carefully watered a patch of leafy greens. The air was dense with humidity, a constant reminder of their subterranean existence. "These cucumbers are looking particularly robust," Brian commented, gesturing towards a vine laden with the green vegetables.

Seo-Yeon smiled, her hand resting on her swollen stomach. "They must know they're about to become pickles." Suddenly, her face contorted. A sharp intake of breath escaped her lips. "Brian," she gasped, her voice tight. "I think...I think my water just broke." Brian's eyes widened. He dropped his pruning shears as if they were on fire. "What? Now? But...but we still have like, a week!" He stammered, his face paling. He knew the baby was due soon, but 'soon' felt a lot more comfortable when it was still 'in the future' and not 'right now'.

Seo-Yeon chuckled despite the obvious discomfort. "Babies don't always read calendars, darling." A trickle of water confirmed her assessment. This was definitely the real deal. Panic warred with a surge of adrenaline in Brian's veins. He scooped Seo-Yeon up into his arms, bridal style, nearly losing his balance in the process. "Hold on tight! We're going upstairs!" "Brian! I can walk!" Seo-Yeon protested, but she wrapped her arms around his neck nonetheless.

He ignored her, his legs pumping as he hurried towards the lift that ascended to the garage. "Nope! Conserving energy! You're about to do all the hard work, I'm just providing transportation." He burst through the door of the infirmary, Seo-Yeon still cradled in his arms. Olivia sat on the chair, engrossed in a dog-eared copy of "US Weekly". She looked up, startled by the sudden intrusion. "Brian? What's going on?" Olivia asked, blinking owlishly. "Seo-Yeon's water broke!" Brian announced, his voice bordering on hysterical. "We need help!"

Olivia's eyes widened. She tossed the magazine aside with surprising speed and instantly switched into nurse mode. "Okay, okay, lay her down on the bed. Brian, go get Andrea. Now! She's probably asleep." He didn't need telling twice. Brian deposited Seo-Yeon as gently as possible onto the bed, his hands hovering nervously. "I'll be right back!" he promised, before bolting out of the infirmary. "And Brian!" Olivia called after him, "Try not to scream too much! We don't want to scare the baby before it's even born!"

Brian practically dragged Andrea into the infirmary, looking like she'd been yanked from a deep sleep, which she had. Her hair was a mess, and she squinted blearily at the scene before her. "Brian, calm down! What on earth...Oh!" Andrea's eyes finally focused on Seo-Yeon, who was breathing rapidly on the bed, her face a mixture of pain and excitement. Olivia was already barking instructions, her earlier airheadedness completely gone.

"Andrea, you're here! Good. I've got the basics covered. Can you check her dilation?" Olivia requested, stepping away from the bed for Andrea to do the checkup. Brian hovered near Seo-Yeon, looking utterly helpless. "Is she...is she okay? Are we okay? What do I do?" He wrung his hands, his voice a high-pitched squeak. Seo-Yeon, despite the obvious discomfort, managed a weak smile. "I'm fine, honey. Just...breathe with me, okay? And maybe find something useful to do besides hyperventilating."

Andrea finished her examination, her expression thoughtful. "She's about four centimeters dilated. It's still early, but things are definitely progressing. Brian, can you grab me a clean set of sheets from the supply closet? And maybe a cool compress for her forehead." Olivia nodded in agreement. "Good call, Andrea. Also, someone needs to alert David. He'll want to know."

Seo-Yeon gasped and squeezed Brian's hand so hard, he thought his fingers might break. "Wait, no David, please!" Tears filled Seo-Yeon's eyes. "I can't do David right now. Maybe later, but not now!" Brian looked from Seo-Yeon to Andrea and Olivia, his face etched with confusion. "But...but David always wants to be involved. He knows so much, and he's... well, he's David."

Andrea, ever the diplomat, knelt beside Seo-Yeon. "Honey, it's okay. Labor can be a very personal experience. If you don't want David here right now, that's perfectly fine. We can handle this." She shot a pointed look at Brian, silently urging him to support his wife's wishes. Olivia, though surprised, quickly adapted. "Yeah, Brian, listen to your wife. We've got this. Besides," she added, "sometimes too many cooks spoil the broth. Let's keep the energy calm and focused, okay?"

Brian looked back at his wife, her face strained but resolute. He could see the genuine fear in her eyes, the vulnerability that she rarely showed. He sighed, his shoulders slumping slightly. "Okay, okay. No David. You're sure?" Seo-Yeon nodded weakly, squeezing his hand again. "Thank you, honey." Brian straightened up, trying to regain some semblance of composure. "Okay, sheets and a compress. Got it." He hesitated, then turned back to Andrea. "But... what about Mom? Or... or Tanya? Should I get one of them?"

Seo-Yeon groaned a little. "Jennifer is too much.. Tanya is okay.." Andrea hummed thoughtfully. "Jennifer might be a bit...enthusiastic for this stage. Tanya could be a good choice, she's got a calming presence, and she can help Seo-Yeon." Olivia chimed in, "Yeah, Tanya would be great. She can give you a massage, Seo-Yeon, help you relax."

Brian nodded. "Okay, Tanya it is. I'll go get her. And the sheets. And the compress. Okay." He took a deep breath, trying to channel some of David's legendary calm. "Okay, I can do this." With a slightly more determined look, he hurried out of the room, leaving Andrea and Olivia to tend to Seo-Yeon.

Brian returned, a stack of clean sheets clutched in his arms like a winning lottery ticket. He deposited them gratefully into Olivia's waiting hands. "Compress next, right?"

189

he asked, mopping his brow with the back of his hand. "Where do we keep the... the... compressy thing?" "Freezer," Andrea replied, pointing with a nod. "Bottom drawer. Try not to eat the ice cream this time."

Brian shot her a look of mock offense. "Hey, that was a stress popsicle! Totally different situation." He hurried off, the image of tooty-frooty briefly distracting him from the impending arrival of his first child. As he rummaged through the freezer, he thought back to Seo-Yeon's adamant request: No David. He understood, of course. David could be a bit... much. Especially during something as personal as childbirth. Plus, David had a habit of turning every situation into a learning opportunity, complete with historical anecdotes and obscure scientific facts. No one needed a history lesson on the evolution of the human pelvis while in labor.

The main house was eerily silent, the only sound the distant beep of Grace's monitor from her room. Brian padded softly up the stairs. He knew Tanya and Elena shared a room closest to the stairs, right across from David's room. As he approached their door, he took a deep breath, trying to compose himself. This isn't exactly the ideal time for a social call, but he wanted to do right by his wife.

He gently pushed the door open, peering into the dimly lit room. Two beds, one on each side of the room. Maybe Tanya's bed was closest to the door? After sneaking close to the bed, he whispered, "Tanya? Hey, Tanya, are you awake? You feeling alright?" He reached out and gently shook her shoulder. A startled groan escaped, and a sleepy voice mumbled, "Ugh... wha...? Brian?" Brian froze, his heart sinking into his stomach. The voice was all wrong. That was definitely Elena, not Tanya.

Brian apologized. "I'm sorry Elena, I was looking for Tanya, I thought you were her." Elena groggily sat up, rubbing her eyes. "All Asian women don't look alike, and that's racist," she snapped, still half-asleep. Brian flushed, feeling embarrassed. "I'm sorry, Elena. It's just... Seo-Yeon is in labor downstairs in the Infirmary, and I'm trying to fetch Tanya for support." Elena rolled her eyes, her tone softening a bit. "Well, I guess I can't blame you for being a bit flustered. "You know, maybe you should get a sign or something," he said, backing away.

Elena chuckled, shaking her head. "That's a good idea. Maybe we could use name tags or something like that." As he was about to leave, Elena pointed at the big Thailand flag hanging over Tanya's bed. "Or you could just look for that." Brian nodded, feeling a bit foolish. "Right. I'll remember that next time. Thanks, Elena." With that, he sneaked close to Tanya's bed and carefully woke her up. "Tanya, it's time. Seo-Yeon is in labor downstairs in the Infirmary, and she needs your support." Tanya sat up, rubbing her eyes sleepily. "Oh, okay. I'll be right there."

Brian burst into the Infirmary, a flustered mess. Andrea, ever the composed nurse, raised an eyebrow at his hurried entrance. Seo-Yeon, lying in the delivery bed, managed a weak smile. "Brian? Everything alright? You look like you walked in on your parents," Andrea said. He ran a hand through his already disheveled hair. "It's...it's Tanya. Or rather, it wasn't Tanya. Oh god, this is going to sound so bad." Seo-Yeon, despite the obvious discomfort of labor, found the energy to giggle. "Did you forget what she looks like, honey?"

Brian groaned. "No! It's just... I went to get Tanya, and it was dark, and I wasn't thinking clearly." He paused to gulp some air before continuing. "It was Elena, not Tanya! I woke up Elena!" Andrea's lips twitched, fighting back a smile. "You woke up Elena? And you think that's a disaster?" "She was not happy," Brian confessed, his face reddening. "She said something about all Asian women not looking alike and that I was a racist... I just wanted to find Tanya quickly."

Seo-Yeon burst out laughing, clutching her stomach, a move she immediately regretted. "Oh Brian, you are unbelievable," she gasped between giggles. "Did you even look for the giant Thailand flag over Tanya's bed?" Brian's face went from red to a shade of purple usually reserved for eggplants. "She pointed that out after the fact! It was dark! And I was stressed! Cut me some slack, Seo-Yeon! Plus, who even does that? Does dad mix them up too?"

"I heard my name," Tanya said, stepping into the infirmary. Her arms crossed, a picture of serene beauty despite the underlying steel in her eyes. "And apparently, I'm being used as an excuse for...mistaken identity?" She glanced pointedly at Brian, who shrunk under her gaze. "For the record, that flag," she gestured with a perfectly manicured nail over her shoulder, presumably toward her bedroom, "was hung specifically because Jessica and Taylor kept putting Elena's clothes in my dresser. Apparently, we all look the same to them, too."

Before the tension could escalate into a full-blown marital spat, the door swung open again, and Elena sauntered in, looking remarkably composed for someone who'd been rudely awakened. "Well, since my name's being dragged through the mud," Elena drawled, her eyes glinting with amusement, "I figured I'd add my two cents. Brian, honey, I appreciate you thinking I'm as gorgeous as Tanya, and she is gorgeous," she added with a wink to Tanya, "but maybe next time, try turning on a light?"

She surveyed the room, her gaze landing on Brian's mortified face. "Honestly, I don't blame you, it's not like Jennifer and Tiffany's room. That's a whole different story. It's practically a historical archive of their... interests. You wouldn't even need light to tell which side of the room is whose. I mean, Jennifer got that sex swing for Christmas, remember? Hard to mistake that."

Brian, face a shade of red previously unseen in nature, grabbed Elena's arm and started steering her towards the door. "Right, Elena, thanks for clearing that up. We'll... continue this discussion later, maybe over some tea?" As Brian practically frog-marched Elena out of the infirmary, the room was filled with an uncomfortable silence. Andrea, ever the professional, cleared her throat. "Right. Back to Seo-Yeon. How are you feeling, dear?"

Seo-Yeon, bless her heart, managed a weak smile. "Better, actually. The excitement seems to have... helped things along." Just then, a wail pierced the air. Not a cry of discomfort, but a full-blown, lungs-exercising scream. "That's Dillon!" Brian yelled from the hallway, momentarily forgetting his personal crisis. He burst back into the room, his face now covered in pure, unadulterated joy. "He's here! He's finally here!"

The tension in the room immediately dissipated, replaced by smiles and relieved sighs. Andrea, Tanya and Olivia converged on Seo-Yeon, their earlier awkwardness forgotten in the face of new life. The focus shifted entirely to the tiny human who had just made his grand entrance into the world.

As Brian held his son for the first time, a wave of overwhelming emotion washed over him. He looked at Tanya, a silent apology etched on his face, then back at Dillon, a fierce protectiveness settling in his eyes. He knew he had to thank everyone who helped, but in that moment, holding his son, everything else seemed to fade away. He remembered David's uncanny way with his children, the way they seemed to understand things others didn't. A wild thought sparked in his mind: What if...?

Taking a deep breath, Brian cleared his throat. He looked down at the screaming infant in his arms and, in a clear, calm tone, addressed Dillon as if he were a miniature adult holding court. "Alright, Dillon," Brian began, his voice surprisingly steady. "I get it. You're here, you're new, and everything's probably terrifying. It's cold out here, there's no functioning civilization, and frankly, your dad has no idea what he's doing. But you were just born, man! You gotta give us a little bit of patience. We're all figuring this out as we go."

Seo-Yeon, still pale but beaming, watched with wide eyes. Tanya raised an eyebrow, but a smile tugged at the corner of her lips. Andrea, ever the practical nurse, simply adjusted the small blanket around Dillon. Olivia, however, seemed to be taking mental notes, like she was going to write a guide for new parents.

Brian, emboldened by the lack of immediate ridicule, continued. "See, you're not alone here, little guy. You've got people who are going to love you, even if they sometimes smell like hay and recycled hydroponics." He carefully brought Dillon closer to Seo-Yeon. "This beautiful, slightly exhausted, woman is your mother. Her name is Seo-Yeon. She just went through a lot to get you here, so maybe dial down the screaming a notch, huh?"

To everyone's utter astonishment, Dillon actually did quiet down. Not completely, mind you, but the shrieks diminished to a series of confused whimpers. "Okay, okay," Brian said, genuinely impressed. "Maybe this talking thing is working." He turned to Tanya, holding Dillon out slightly. "And this is your Aunt Tanya. She's the cool one."

Tanya leaned in, her eyes soft as she studied the tiny face. Dillon, in turn, seemed to be trying his best to focus on her features, his gaze unfocused but clearly intent. "We promise," Brian continued, his voice softening even further, "if you give us a chance to understand what you're saying, we won't treat you like a worm in a blanket. We'll try to figure out what all the screaming is about."

He paused, then asked Dillon the most fundamental question of all: "Are you hungry?" Dillon, seemingly understanding the sheer gravitas of the question, responded with a single, decisive grunt. "Alright, alright, understood,"

Brian said quickly, relief flooding his face. He carefully passed Dillon back to Seo-Yeon. "Food is the answer, as always."

As Seo-Yeon began to settle Dillon into her arms for feeding, Brian suddenly remembered something. "Oh! And your grandpa David is upstairs asleep." The effect was instantaneous. Dillon, who had been snuffling contentedly against Seo-Yeon, stilled completely. His unfocused eyes widened, and his body relaxed completely.

Olivia, watching from the corner, gasped quietly and covered her mouth with her hand, tears welling in her eyes. She had always wondered if David's connection to his children extended to his grandchildren, and this... this was proof. The boy had never met his grandfather, yet the mere mention of David's name had snapped him to attention.

Tanya noticed Olivia's distress and squeezed her arm gently. "Are you alright, Olivia?" she whispered. Olivia nodded, unable to speak, a mixture of awe and emotion washing over her. Seo-Yeon, completely bewildered, looked from Dillon to Brian and back again. "What... just happened?"

Tanya smiled knowingly. "It's alright, Seo-Yeon. Dillon is a biological inheritor of David's... life. He carries a piece of David within him, just like Brian does. The mention of David's name probably feels... familiar. Comforting, even." She paused, considering. "Think of it like a very faint echo of David resonating within him."

Seo-Yeon's eyes widened in understanding. "So, it's like... a baby-sized version of David's brain recognizing someone important?" Tanya chuckled, "Something like that.

It's… complicated." She glanced at Olivia's tear-streaked face, a silent understanding passing between them.

Meanwhile, outside, the sounds of hammering and cheerful complaining filled the humid air. Caleb, Darrel, Andrew and Riley were hard at work on the new pig enclosure, an ambitious extension to the existing barn. "Remind me again why we're building a pig palace at two in the morning?" Riley asked, wiping a bead of sweat from her brow.

Andrew chuckled, adjusting his grip on a heavy beam. "Because David wants happy pigs. Happy pigs make good bacon. Good bacon makes David happy. And when David's happy, we're all happy. Plus, it's better than building it in the middle of the afternoon."

Darrel snorted. "Sounds about right. The sooner we finish, the better." Caleb, who had been working in near silence, finally spoke up. "It's not a bad gig. We get to be the secret behind our own success. I mean, did you see Thomas's face when we finished up yesterday? Dude thought this ranch was run by elves or something."

Riley rolled her eyes playfully. "We're new to this, just like he is, you know." She paused, considering his perspective. "But I see your point, he doesn't know everything, and if he thinks we helped build this place from the ground up, that's more leverage for when we have to help out at the settlements." "Speaking of settlements," Andrew said, carefully placing the beam. "We gotta start thinking about that rotation to Eli's settlements. Josh and Lily are probably ready to come back."

"Yeah, my turn's coming up," Darrel said, sighing. "Me and Reagan are heading out next week. Not exactly a vacation, is it?" "Better you than me," Riley said, grinning. "I hear Eli's managed to find more volunteers. Plus, you're good with people, Darrel. You can charm the pants off anyone." "Except Eli himself," Darrel muttered. "That guy gives me the creeps. Always staring. Makes you feel like you're trespassing on his lawn."

Caleb nodded in agreement. "He's a bit... intense. But he's learning. David wouldn't put us out there if he didn't think it was necessary. Eli needs help, and so do those settlements. They need to learn how to be self-sufficient." Darrel added, "The most important thing is that they learn to work together. Most people are just naturally selfish. They have to learn that sharing and helping each other is how they're going to survive."

A comfortable silence descended as they worked, the rhythmic hammering and sawing punctuated by the occasional grunts of exertion. Caleb, never one to leave a thread dangling, broke the quiet. "Hey Riley, what's the deal with the apartment renovations? I heard some rumblings."

Riley wiped sweat from her brow with the back of her hand. "Callie was trying to earn brownie points from Junior by saving materials. She thinks she can get on his good side by being super efficient." Caleb raised an eyebrow, a playful smirk spreading across his face. "And is it working?"

"I don't know," Riley admitted, shrugging. "She's really thrown herself into the project. Besides, she's probably in the apartment with Junior right now, and Emma, so...

yeah." "Callie and Emma are with Junior?" Darrel repeated. "Framing walls, huh? That sounds like a euphemism if I ever heard one."

Riley playfully shoved his shoulder. "Get your mind out of the gutter, Darrel. They're literally framing walls. Aidan's got a plan for those apartments, and he needs all the help he can get." "Speaking of Junior and efficiency…" Caleb trailed off, his voice laced with amusement. "Is Callie…you know… involved with him?"

Riley sighed dramatically, the picture of exasperation. "I don't know if he's sleeping with Callie! And frankly, it's none of my business. Or yours! What Junior does with his time is his own affair, as long as everyone is happy and safe." Darrel, never one to let a juicy rumor die, pressed on. "So you're saying you wouldn't be surprised?"

Riley threw her hands up in the air. "I'm saying I genuinely don't care! Look, I get plenty of attention from Junior, okay? And one more wouldn't hurt. The man has a lot of love to give. And if Callie gets a piece of that, good for her. I like Callie. She's fun, she's smart, and she actually seems to enjoy hauling lumber and swinging a hammer. Plus, Junior seems to like her too. He likes having people around him who are enthusiastic and willing to work."

Andrew, who had been mostly silent during this exchange, chuckled. "Sounds like we're all just trying to survive and find a little happiness wherever we can get it. Even if that means building a pigpen at two in the morning." Riley nodded, a thoughtful expression on her face. "Exactly. And if that happiness involves a few extra hands on deck…

well, who am I to judge?" She winked at Darrel. "Besides, you're going to be too busy charming Eli's settlers to worry about Junior's love life."

Darrel, however, wasn't easily deterred. He leaned closer to Riley, lowering his voice conspiratorially. "But is he... you know... like David? Willing to, uh, take one of his wives at a moment's notice?" He waggled his eyebrows suggestively.

Riley's lips curved into a mischievous smile. "Oh, Darrel," she purred, a playful glint dancing in her eyes. "He absolutely is. And it's quite... exciting." She leaned in, her voice dropping to a whisper. "All that protocol training David put us through? It really taught me that yielding to your master can be... the most rewarding thing."

Darrel's jaw dropped. "Master? You call Junior 'Master'?" He looked genuinely shocked, the picture of a street thug momentarily disoriented. Riley chuckled, a low, throaty sound. "That's a side of Junior only his wives get to enjoy, sweetie. He's a protector, a leader, a provider... and sometimes, a Dom. It's all part of the package."

Darrel, still reeling, sputtered, "But... but I just thought... you seemed so... independent." "Independent women can have needs too, Darrel," Riley said with a wink. "And Junior is very good at fulfilling them." She paused, a wicked glint in her eye. "Tell you what. I'll prove it to you." Darrel blinked. "Prove it?" "Yep," Riley said, grabbing her hammer. "I'm going to take a quick break. Need to... re-energize. I'll be right back." She tossed her hammer to

Andrew, gave Darrel a knowing smirk, and sauntered into the nearby work shed.

A few moments later, the shed door creaked open, and Emma emerged. She was wearing the same work clothes as Riley, her face slightly flushed, but her expression was calm and collected. She picked up the hammer seemingly without missing a beat and took Riley's place at the pigpen construction.

Darrel stared, his mouth agape. "What... what just happened?" he stammered. Emma, without looking up from her work, simply said, "Riley needed a break. I'm covering for her. We work as a team, remember? Walls are going up a lot easier than I thought," Emma said, her voice matter-of-fact as she pounded a nail home with a satisfying thwack.

Darrel, still reeling from whatever just transpired, could only manage a weak, "Oh. Good. That's... good." He stumbled over his words, feeling like he'd walked into a bizarre alternate reality show. He wasn't entirely sure what he'd expected to happen when Riley went into that shed, but it definitely wasn't that.

Caleb, ever the observer, chuckled softly. "So, Emma, is Riley just as... strong-willed with Junior as she is with everyone else? Or does she, uh, tone it down a bit?" He asked, clearly enjoying Darrel's visible discomfort. Emma paused. "Why is our relationship always in the tabloids?" she muttered, before fixing Caleb with a playful glare. "You know, you'd think people would have more exciting things to gossip about after the apocalypse, but no, it's always about Junior and his wives.

Honestly, it's like we're the Kardashians of the bunker." She sighed dramatically, then leaned in conspiratorially. "Okay, fine, I'll bite. The truth is, Riley is the complete opposite with Junior. It's... surprising, actually." Darrel's eyebrows shot up. "Surprising how?" "Think of it like this," Emma continued, choosing her words carefully. "Riley's like a wild, untamed mustang in every other aspect of her life. She's got fire, she's got independence, she's got sass for days. But with Junior..." She paused, a soft smile playing on her lips. "With Junior, she's like a stray kitten being rescued from a storm. She lets her guard down."

Caleb nodded thoughtfully. "Yeah, I get it. Junior's got that whole protector vibe going on. He's like, the ultimate safe space." Emma nodded in agreement. "Exactly. He's earned her trust, her vulnerability. Privately," she lowered her voice, "Riley is actually a very sensitive person. She's been through a lot, and sometimes she needs someone to just hold her and tell her everything is going to be okay. Junior does that for her."

Darrel's expression softened. He'd seen Riley's tough exterior, the way she could stare down anyone with a sarcastic quip and a raised eyebrow. He hadn't considered what might lie beneath that facade. "So it's not just... some kind of weird... power thing?" he asked hesitantly.

Emma laughed. "Oh, there's definitely a power thing involved," she grinned, looking at Caleb. "But it's more about trust and understanding than domination. Think of it as... consensual control. It's a release for her, a way to express a part of herself that she doesn't usually show." Caleb snorted. "Consensual control. Sounds kinky."

Darrel leaned on his hammer. "Speaking of... our busy bee, Riley. What do you reckon she's up to right now? Back at the apartment, I mean." Emma's smile turned positively wicked. She leaned in closer, lowering her voice. "Oh, she's definitely not hammering drywall. Knowing Riley? She's probably...fucking our husband right now."

Caleb choked on a laugh, nearly dropping the piece of lumber he was holding. "Emma! You can't just say that!" "Why not?" Emma shrugged innocently. "It's the truth! And besides," she added with a playful wink, "it's not like either of you haven't entertained the very same thought." Darrel couldn't deny it. The thought of Riley, with her fiery energy and untamed spirit, submitting to Junior's control was both intriguing and... well, a little arousing, if he was being honest.

Caleb shifted the conversation. "What about Callie? She was helping Junior with... stuff. Is Riley jealous? Does she care?" Emma considered for a moment, tapping her chin thoughtfully. "Riley? Jealous? Nah. Not when it comes to Junior. Besides," she added with a sly smirk, "Riley isn't shy in front of Callie. Especially since Callie wants in too. And Riley? She's all for it. The more, the merrier, right?"

A moment of silence hung in the air before Darrel, broke the quiet. "So... what do you think of Callie? Besides the obvious... you know..." He gestured vaguely towards his chest. Emma grinned. "Oh, Callie's great. She's got perky tits, that's for sure. But she's also got a heart of gold. She's always willing to help out, she's got a killer sense of humor, and she's fiercely loyal to Junior. And honestly?" Emma paused, her eyes sparkling with anticipation. "I'm excited to see what Callie looks like after getting her pussy blasted by our husband." Darrel and Caleb exchanged a look, their expressions a mixture of shock and amusement. Emma was definitely not one for subtlety.

Chapter 36:

The Rebirth of Kyle

Grace was propped up against a mountain of pillows, her face pale but her eyes bright. Each breath was a shallow, carefully measured thing, a constant reminder of the bullet that had torn through her lung barely two weeks ago. Andrea, bless her heart, had transformed his little apartment into a makeshift recovery room, complete with an IV stand and a bewildering array of medical supplies. "Easy there, Grace," Kyle murmured, gently adjusting her pillows. "Don't try to talk too much." "But...bored," she rasped, her voice barely audible. "So...bored."

Kyle chuckled, a sound that was perhaps a little too loud in the small space. "I know, sweetheart. But you need to rest. Think of it as...forced relaxation." "Forced...torture," Grace corrected, a faint smile playing on her lips. He squeezed her hand, his gaze softening. Seeing her like this, so fragile and vulnerable, still stirred a potent cocktail of anger and protectiveness inside him. He understood that Thomas had made a mistake, that he hadn't intended to hurt Grace specifically, but the image of her collapsing after the shot echoed in his nightmares.

Just then, the door creaked open, revealing David and Seth. David held a laundry basket overflowing with Grace's clothes. Seth, his teenage face a mixture of awkwardness and something that might have been amusement, trailed behind.

Kyle immediately started to push himself up from the edge of the bed, sling and all. "David, I can get that…"

David held up a hand, stopping him in his tracks. "Whoa there, son. You so much as think about getting out of that bed again, and I'll break your legs myself." He punctuated the threat with a gentle, but firm, setting down of the basket. "I figured Grace would want her things here, make it feel more…homely." Grace frowned, her brow furrowing slightly. "But…why? I'm just here to recover. I'll be back in my room in a month or so, right?"

David exchanged a knowing glance with Seth. "Well, honey, I was thinking…seeing as how you two went through hell and considering the…circumstances…it might be easier if you just stayed here. Indefinitely." Grace's eyes widened. "Indefinitely? But…Dad, you have a rule! No cohabitation until you're married!" She looked at Kyle, then back at David, her expression a mixture of confusion and dawning realization.

Seth, seizing the moment with the grace of a newborn giraffe, popped a small confetti popper, sending a pathetic shower of multi-colored paper raining down on them. Then announced in a flat, monotone voice, "Congratulations to the bride and groom." The silence that followed was so thick, it could clog a toilet. Kyle, his face a mask of conflicted emotions, spoke up. "Wait, hold on a minute. What about everyone else? I mean, we can't just… upend everything. We're part of a community here, David." He gestured weakly with his good arm. "People have expectations, feelings…"

David, unfazed by the sudden shift in dynamic, fixed Kyle with a gaze that could melt... maybe, really thick aluminum foil. "Kyle, listen to me. The first person in this entire ranch to make so much as a backhanded comment, a snide remark, or even think a sideways thought about this arrangement, will be cleaning pig shit until Grace here is eighteen years old. And I mean every ounce of pig shit. By hand.

Then, as if switching gears entirely, he smiled. "Besides," he added, his voice laced with a hint of amusement, "I already conferred with the matriarchal council and made the announcement at the meeting on Friday. And let me tell you, nobody was surprised. So, get over yourself. You're not on the front page of the tabloids anymore."

Grace's eyes widened again, this time in abject horror. "You did what?!" "Now, now, sweetheart," David chuckled, waving a dismissive hand. "Don't get your bandages in a bunch. This isn't an announcement of marriage, per se. More of a...declared pairing. An inevitability. You two clearly care for each other. You've been through a traumatic event together. And frankly," he paused, a twinkle in his eye, "you're always at Kyle's apartment anyway. It's just making it official."

Seth, still hovering near the door like an awkward punctuation mark, decided to contribute again. "Yeah, Mom says you practically live here already. Except for, you know, sleeping. So now it would be weird if you weren't together." Grace's brow furrowed, her voice a raspy whisper. "Daddy, what... what has been going on while I've been, you know..." she gestured weakly at her chest, "...trying not to die?"

David stroked his chin thoughtfully. "Well, nothing too earth-shattering. Except, perhaps, for our little 'declared pairing' here. I have been meaning to sit down with you and Kyle here to discuss it privately but... circumstances demanded expediency. Also, Bonnie's been running around making a nuisance of herself and I've been busy. I'm not a miracle worker"

Seth, sensing the conversational lull, perked up. "Oh! Oh! Bonnie's been, like, way more shameless with her kissing. I was setting up before class last week, and she was all tongue-in-mouth with her greeting, in front of everyone. It was so embarrassing!" He shuddered dramatically. David chuckled. "Ah, young love. Or, at least, young... enthusiasm. Speaking of questionable romantic choices, Junior is definitely banging Callie. No doubt about it. Riley seems to be... encouraging her to keep being the mistress. Says it 'makes things spicy.' I swear, that wife of his... she has a penchant for drama, almost as acute as Jennifer." Grace's eyes widened. "Callie? Seriously? I'm not surprised considering how long she has been flirting with him. You're being serious about the mistress thing though?" David nodded.

Seth, ever the eager participant, piped up again. "Actually, Mia has been helping Mom a lot with the hydroponics. And she makes really, really good tortillas! You gotta try them when you're feeling better." Grace's brow furrowed further. "Mia? Who's Mia?" David sighed, running a hand over his head. "Right. You haven't met Mia. She's

Noah's... wife." "Wife?!" Grace looked genuinely shocked, her breath catching in her throat.

David cleared his throat. "It's a long story. She's kind of a refugee, a beautiful Mexican girl from San Antonio. She was part of one of Eli's settlements. The ones we went to when we went to go find Thomas. We went scorched earth. Wiped them out." A flicker of understanding, mixed with horror, crossed Grace's face. "You... wiped them out? What do you mean?" David cleared his throat. The first settlement was just full of people dumb enough to pick a fight. The second was much worse."

He looked at Seth before continuing. "They were selling women as commodities, disgusting business. Mia was the youngest, still... untouched. She was probably like a bar of gold to those animals. Noah and I... well, Seth and I, to be precise, set Noah up as the hero. Once everyone was wiped out, we sent him in to smooth things over. He comforted them, and Isabella basically threw Mia at him as a reward. It was... sweet."

He paused, a wry smile tugging at the corner of his lips. "But it turned out for the best, because Mia really likes Noah, and they've been going at it like rabbits. I swear, I haven't seen Noah so happy in months. It's good for him." Seth nodded enthusiastically. "Yeah! She's always giggling and smiling. And she's trying to learn English. She asks me stuff all the time, like '¿Cómo se dice 'chicken'?' It's really cute."

Grace, still trying to process the whirlwind of information, managed a weak smile. "Does Noah know Spanish?" "Yep," David replied, popping the 'p'. "Learned it in high school. Plus, it was part of his Army training. He's been brushing up too. They spend hours talking...or whatever they do with their hands." He winked, and Seth burst out laughing. "So, she's living here now?" Grace asked. "Sure is!" David said, clapping his hands together as if declaring the matter settled. "Sharing a room with Noah, and she's fitting in great. Everyone loves her. Even Jessica, and you know how picky she can be."

He paused, a thought striking him. "Speaking of additions, you haven't even heard the latest! Brian and Seo-Yeon had their baby! It's a boy, they named him Dillon. Which means we now have five babies in the family! Five!" He puffed out his chest with pride. Kyle chuckled. "Yeah, the place is starting to feel like a daycare center. Aidan's been going crazy trying to baby-proof everything, though I think Dillon is more likely to cause problems once he's mobile."

David waved a dismissive hand. "It'll be fine, he's a Renado. The first one with Black hair I might add." He turned serious again. "Enough about local events, how are you feeling, Grace? Really?" Grace swallowed hard, her voice a raspy whisper. "It's... alright. Aches, but I can handle it. More worried about Kyle's arm." "Don't you worry about me," Kyle said, squeezing her hand. "I'm just glad you're... you know..." He trailed off, unable to articulate the relief. "Alive?" Seth offered helpfully, snapping his fingers. Kyle glared at him. "Yeah, alive, thank you professor."

"Thomas?" Grace rasped, the word catching in her throat. "He's...here?" David nodded. "He is. Living in the garage, for now." "The garage?" Grace's brows furrowed.

"He's not…down in the bunkers?" "Nope. He's got a cot set up under the main house. He doesn't get such privileges. He needs to see the kind of life he almost took from you." David reiterated, his voice hardening slightly. "He needs to understand the weight of his actions. Look, Grace, whether he lives or dies… that's your call. It shouldn't be my decision."

Kyle shifted uncomfortably, adjusting the sling on his arm. "David…" David held up a hand, silencing Kyle with a look. "This isn't about revenge, Kyle. This is about justice. About Thomas understanding the consequences of his choices." He turned back to Grace, his gaze softening. "He's been working with everyone. Tending to the animals, helping build that new pig pen…you know, honest work. Not glamorous, but necessary." Seth, surprisingly serious, added his two cents. "He actually doesn't complain much. He just does what he's told, keeps his head down."

Grace chewed on her lip, considering this information. She didn't hate Thomas, not really. Disappointed? Absolutely. Angry? Sure. But hate felt like a waste of energy, especially in their current reality. "He shot Kyle, David. Almost killed him." "I know, Grace. And he's currently serving time, waiting for his sentencing." David's voice was gentle but firm. "He's seeing the family he nearly destroyed. He's seeing the community he almost ripped apart. We're not working him to the bone. The point isn't punishment. The point is to show him the life he tried to take from you, the kind of people that would be hurt by your death. And once he's attached, and if you decide to spare him, we can send him back to Eli."

Kyle let out a snort. "Send him back? You think Eli will be thrilled to get him back after he cost him half his people?" "Eli won't be putting him in the penthouse, that's for sure." David chuckled, then his expression turned serious again. "But that's Eli's problem. Our problem is making sure Thomas understands the gravity of what he did." Grace sighed, exhaustion creeping in. "What if… what if I just want him gone?" David stepped closer, taking her hand. "Then he's gone, sweetheart. Your word is judgement.

Grace's eyes fell to her hands. "Daddy, do you know why he did it?" David thought for a moment before answering. "Honestly, pumpkin. I just think he was trying to help Eli. I mean, he was seventeen when everything fell apart, and I doubt he had a very good role model growing up." David turned his eyes to Seth. "Then Eli came along, probably thought he was some kind of prophet. But Eli's no leader. He's just a well-prepared survivor. Not to mention the bozos at the other settlements." He glanced at Kyle, then at Grace. "He probably thought he was rescuing you. From… us."

Kyle scoffed. "Rescuing her? By shooting her?" David held up a hand, silencing Kyle again. "I think he was removing an obstacle, and you were the biggest one. Plus, logic doesn't always play a part in these things. Fear, desperation, misplaced loyalty… they can all cloud judgment. Thomas is young, impressionable. And clearly, he made a terrible mistake." He turned back to Grace, his voice softer. "The question is, what do we do with that mistake?"

Grace's voice was barely a whisper, a rasping sound strained by the lingering pain. "What do you want to do, Daddy?" David steepled his fingers, a familiar gesture that betrayed the gears turning in his mind. "I want him to experience what he was so willing to destroy. The community, the comfort, the… vibes, as you young people say." A ghost of a smile touched his lips.

He continued, his voice gaining strength. "I want Thomas to know what it feels like to be part of something bigger than himself, something good. To share a meal without suspicion, to work towards a common goal, to laugh without fear. We work hard, yes, but we also take care of each other. We're not just surviving, we're living."

He paused, letting his words sink in. "Then, when he goes back to Eli, he'll have seen the difference. He'll have felt it. And it'll leave a longing, a yearning for something he can't easily get back. He'll have to earn it. He'll have to work to build that kind of community for himself and others." Kyle, nursing his wounded shoulder, shifted uncomfortably. "So, you're saying we're just… what? Letting him have a vacation here? He shot us, David! He almost killed Grace!" His voice still tight with suppressed anger.

David turned his calm, unwavering gaze to Kyle. "I understand your anger, Kyle. Believe me, I do. But revenge won't rebuild what was broken. We need to break the cycle of violence, not perpetuate it. If we can show Thomas a better way, a more fulfilling way, then maybe, just maybe, we can prevent him from ever making such a mistake again. He is still a child, Kyle. Misguided, definitely, but still capable of learning."

Seth, who had been silent, his young face etched with concern for Grace, finally spoke. "But... how? How do you just let him... be here? After what he did?" David sighed. "It's not easy, Seth. And it requires a leap of faith. But we'll keep him busy. We'll give him tasks, responsibilities. We'll show him what it means to contribute, to be valued. And more importantly, we'll show him what he's missing." Kyle frowned, suspicion clouding his eyes. "Okay, but what has he even seen here so far? Just the outside stuff, right? He hasn't been inside the main house much, has he?"

David nodded slowly. "That's right, Kyle. He works outside, primarily in the smithy, helping with the pigs, or he's helping in the barn. He comes inside the main house or work shed occasionally, fetching tools or delivering supplies. But he hasn't seen the bunkers. Never been further than the generator room. That remains my domain, and I have no intention for him to have access to it."

He continued, a subtle steel entering his voice. "Because if Thomas gets to look under the skirt, he might get greedy. He might see our resources, our infrastructure, and decide that Eli needs it more than we do. That's a risk I'm not willing to take. He needs to see the fruits of our labor, not the foundations upon which they are built." David's grinned widened. "Plus, think of the loyalty he'll harbor for us in the future."

Kyle leaned back against the headboard of the bed, wincing slightly at the movement. "It's... devious, isn't it?

You're basically dangling heaven in front of him, then you're going to drop him back to earth with nothing. But I admit, it's... surprisingly more sustainable. Way more sustainable than just locking him up or killing him." He looked at Grace who was resting beside him, her face pale but her eyes bright. "It's... messed up, but I get it."

Just then, a knock sounded on the door. Andrea entered, carrying an IV bag. "Morning, everyone," she said with a warm smile. "Time for your antibiotics, Grace. And let's have a look at that bandage." She expertly hooked up the saline, then checked the catheter in her arm. As the clear fluid began to drip, Grace asked, her voice soft, "Andrea, how long am I going to be... like this?" She gestured weakly to her bandaged arm.

Andrea examined Grace's arm with a gentle touch. "It's going to take time, sweetie. A gunshot wound is serious, especially one as extensive as yours. A few months, maybe? It depends on how well you heal. We'll keep a close eye on it, make sure there's no infection. Plenty of rest, good food, and keeping that arm still are key." "Messed up doesn't even cover it," Kyle muttered, running a hand through his hair. "David's got the patience of a saint, or maybe a sociopath, I can't decide which."

Grace squeezed his hand. "He's just... trying to make something good out of it. For everyone." She winced as Andrea adjusted her arm. "Andrea, is there... any chance of scarring? I mean, I know it's stupid, but..." Andrea patted her hand reassuringly. "We're doing everything we can to minimize it, honey. I'll be applying Mederma, it minimizes

215

scarring when applied in fresh wounds, daily. There might be a small one, but it'll fade over time. You're young, you heal fast."

David stepped forward. "Andrea's right, Grace. Your age is a significant advantage. You still have remarkable tissue regeneration capabilities, something that diminishes considerably as we get older. We'll keep you slathered in all the right stuff, to help with the scarring." He turned to Kyle. "The entry wound on Grace will be minimal, practically invisible. And the incision to remove the bullet was made discreetly, under her left breast, she might not even notice it. You, on the other hand," David said with a smile, "will have a lasting souvenir on the front of your shoulder."

Before Kyle could retort, a flurry of little footsteps echoed from the hallway, followed by gentle knocks. The door opened, and Beth, Lori, Janet, Mike and Bonnie filed in, their faces a mix of concern and curiosity. "Miss Grace! How are you feeling?" Beth asked, her voice filled with genuine concern. Lori, ever the practical one, added, "We brought you some drawing supplies. To keep you busy." She held up a stack of colored pencils and a sketchbook.

Janet placed a hand on Grace's leg. "We're going to miss you in class today, darling. I told them they could do free reading, but they all wanted to come see you." Mike, looking slightly awkward, mumbled, "Hope you get better soon." Grace, still a little pale but radiating warmth, surprised Mike by pulling him into a hug, kissing him on the cheek. "Thank you, Mike," she said, her voice soft but clear. "You were so brave saving my life in the car. I'm really proud of you." Mike blushed, his awkwardness intensifying tenfold. He muttered something unintelligible, shuffling his feet and avoiding eye contact. Andrea chuckled softly, ruffling his hair.

Meanwhile, Bonnie, with the single-minded focus of a heat-seeking missile, had zeroed in on Seth. She bypassed all pleasantries and, without a word, marched directly to him. Seth, who had been standing stiffly beside David, simply stood there. She then proceeded to wrap his arms around her waist, pressing her back against him in what she evidently considered her "rightful place." Seth, used to her antics, simply locked his hands together.

When Janet started ushering the kids out of the room, Seth simply followed. "Learning doesn't stop, just because Grace got shot," he said pointedly, guiding Bonnie by the shoulders toward the door. David, ever the perceptive one, took the cue. "Alright, you two lovebirds," he boomed, a twinkle in his eye. "I won't take up any more of your time. You need rest, and Kyle's got to keep that shoulder from rusting shut." He leaned down, kissed Grace on the forehead, a tender, fatherly gesture, then offered Kyle a firm fist bump. "Get well soon, both of you." With that, he turned and strode out of the room, leaving the two recovering patients alone again.

The silence that followed was thick with unspoken thoughts. Kyle shifted in his chair, trying to find a comfortable position that didn't tug at the healing wound in his shoulder. Grace watched him, her brow furrowed in concern. "You okay?" she asked softly. "Yeah, yeah, just peachy," Kyle replied, his voice a little strained. "Feels like someone's got a rusty nail hammered into my shoulder, but other than that, I'm golden." He managed a weak smile.

Grace returned the smile, though her eyes remained serious. "Hey Kyle?" she asked, suddenly thoughtful. "You've been around Dad for a while now. So, I was wondering, how do you see him, as a father-in-law, a boss, or as a brother-in-law?" Kyle paused, considering the question. It was a layered one, and his relationship with David was equally complex. He wasn't just his fiancé's father; he was the leader of their community, a man Kyle respected deeply. But there was something more there too, a connection that went beyond the hierarchical structure of their lives.

He took a long swig of his iced tea. "Well, that's... complicated, Grace. Trying to fit David in any one box, is like trying to put a tornado in a mason jar. "He was my brother-in-law first, right? When he married Kayla. I gotta admit, Jason and I had some serious doubts back then. I mean, Kayla getting a divorce because Kevin was cheating, and then she jumps right into a relationship with a guy who already has, like, six wives at the time? We were picturing all sorts of drama, the kind you see in those ridiculous reality shows." He chuckled dryly. "Turns out, David's about as far from a reality TV star as you can get."

Grace nodded, understanding dawning in her eyes. "So, brother-in-law... but with reservations?" "Yeah, big reservations. Then he hired Jason and me to teach Junior gunsmithing. That made him my boss. But not just any boss, you know? It's not like clocking in and out at some factory. He's... David. He's got this way of making you feel like you're working with him, not for him. Kyle sighed dramatically. "And now, he's about to be my father-in-law. Which... well, it's still sinking in. Seems like just yesterday I was deciding which flavor of ramen I could make into the most dishes, and now I'm engaged to the daughter of probably the smartest, most prepared, and most... multi-married man in Texas."

He leaned back against the headboard, looking up at the ceiling. "It's a lot to process, Grace. He's not just a father-in-law; he's like... the wise, all-knowing patriarch of this whole operation. He's the guy who keeps everything running, who makes the tough decisions, who somehow manages to keep nine wives happy without starting World War III." Grace laughed, reaching over to take his hand. "Hey! Don't forget his daughters! And his sons! We're a handful too, you know." "Believe me, I know," Kyle said, grinning. "But seriously, Grace, it's more than all those labels. He's... he's David. He's... sui generis, you know? He's his own thing. Trying to define him with just one word is impossible."

He shifted slightly. "And honestly, you're not that different, Grace. You, Seth, Junior, Aidan, Brian, Lily... all of you. Nobody sees you all as just children. You're not just kids hanging around the ranch. You're all, well, let's be real, you're like generals in his army. Each of you has your own theater, your own mission, your own way of leading and contributing to this whole, wild, incredible thing he's built."

Grace's cheeks flushed a delicate pink at the unexpected praise. She hadn't really thought of herself that way, not consciously. She just existed, helping where she could, learning what David taught her, and trying her best.

But hearing Kyle say it, seeing the earnestness in his eyes… it made her feel something deep and warm settle in her chest. "Generals, huh?" she mused, a small, thoughtful smile replacing her earlier mirth. "Sounds a bit grand, doesn't it? But I guess… I guess I see what you mean." She paused, her gaze drifting. "Still, even generals have their weaknesses. Or in my case, annoying injuries."

She shifted, letting out a soft sigh, her eyes clouding with a hint of petulant frustration. "God, the worst thing about getting shot, besides the actual getting shot part and the pain, is that we can't… you know. Fuck." Kyle's breath hitched for a split second, a surprised chuckle rumbling in his chest. His eyes widened slightly, then softened with understanding and a touch of shared frustration. He squeezed her hand again, his thumb stroking her knuckles. "Yeah, I know. It sucks. But hey, your body's got to heal, right? Don't worry about it too much right now. We've got plenty of time for that later. For now, it's all about getting you back to 100%."

Grace pouted playfully, her lower lip sticking out. "Easy for you to say. You're mostly healed up. At least you can… think about it without feeling like you're going to pop a lung." She paused, then a mischievous glint sparkled in her eyes, replacing the pout. She leaned a little closer, lowering her voice, as if the walls of their apartment might listen. "So… if I can't, and you're feeling… recovered enough… do you want a handjob?"

Kyle blinked, caught off guard. A flush crept up his neck, and he found himself staring at the ceiling again, trying to suppress a groan of both desire and pain. "Grace," he said, his voice a little strained, "that's... very sweet of you to offer, especially since you're the one who's worse off, but..." He shifted again, grimacing. "My shoulder, honey. It just... it hurts too much to enjoy anything like that right now, even if I was just lying there. Seriously, the movement, the pressure... it would just be agony. Plus," he added, looking back at her, his expression softening with genuine concern, "you really shouldn't be exerting yourself. Not even for that."

He reached out, lightly touching her cheek. "Just rest, okay? We'll get back to all the fun stuff when we're both mended. Promise. And then we'll make up for lost time, twice over." He leaned in, pressing a soft kiss to her forehead. "You're recovering, that's what matters." Grace sighed, a small, wistful sound, but a faint smile touched her lips. "Fine, fine. I get it. No heroics from the general, even for a good cause." She snuggled closer, resting her head against his chest. She could feel the steady beat of his heart. "It's just... frustrating. We just started having sex like… seven weeks ago. Now we have to wait longer than that to do it again. It's not fair."

A comfortable silence settled between them for a moment. Grace traced a pattern on Kyle's shirt, her thoughts drifting. "Kyle?" she asked, her voice quiet. "Hmm?" "When… when we get married," she began, a slight hesitation in her voice, "what about names? Should I be Grace Myers? Or… should you be Kyle Renado?"

Kyle blinked, caught completely off guard. He'd been anticipating more playful attempts at advanced physical therapy, not a discussion on post-apocalyptic nomenclature. He found himself staring at the ceiling again, not this time to suppress pain, but to organize his thoughts. He hadn't even considered the surname question in this new context. It felt like such a... before concern.

"Renado, huh?" he mused aloud, his brow furrowing slightly in thought. He remembered Josh had chosen to take Renado, believing in David's legacy more than his father's name. It hadn't struck Kyle as a significant act at the time, but he hadn't fully processed the implications for himself. "Yeah. I mean, David's the Patriarch, right? And... well, it's his family we're essentially joining. His vision. His... rebirth," Kyle said. "And you know what Renado means, right? It's from Latin, 'Renatus.' Means 'born again' or 'reborn,'" Grace added.

A lightbulb flickered on in Kyle's mind, illuminating a concept that had been vaguely nascent. "Reborn," he repeated, the word tasting different on his tongue now. He looked at Grace, past the immediate pain, past the boredom, to something larger. "You know," he began, choosing his words carefully, "it's funny. Back before the blackout, it was always about who kept whose name, or hyphenating, or whatever. All about tradition, or equality, or keeping your professional identity. But now..." He shifted, finding a less painful position, and then looked directly at Grace. "Now it's not really about wives and husbands taking each other's last name anymore, is it? Not in the traditional sense, anyway."

Grace tilted her head, listening intently. "What do you mean?" "I mean, look at us. Look at this whole place," Kyle gestured vaguely. "We're not just surviving. David's building something. A new way of life. A... a society, almost. From the ground up. And everyone here, we're all part of it. We all believe in it, or we wouldn't be here."

He took a deep breath. "Josh took the name because he believed in David's legacy. Not just David as a person, but what he represents, what he's building. And 'Renado'... 'born again,' 'reborn'... that's not just David's family name, Grace. That's what we all are. We're reborn into this new world, especially David. Every single one of us who found our way here, who chose to stay and contribute, we're part of a new beginning." He looked at her, a profound earnestness in his eyes, softened by a genuine smile. "It's about unifying under a cause. A purpose. This isn't just David's family; it's becoming the family. The one that's going to rebuild. And 'Rebirth'... well, that seems pretty damn appropriate, doesn't it?"

Grace stared at him, her eyes wide, absorbing his words. The shift in perspective was profound. It wasn't about traditional marriage or personal identity; it was about collective destiny. A unity. "So..." she finally said, a slow smile spreading over her face. "You're saying... Kyle Renado has a nice ring to it?"

Kyle let out a soft laugh. "I'm saying," he corrected, leaning in to kiss her forehead again, "that it's a decision we make together, about what we want to signify. But yeah, if it means committing to this new beginning, to David's vision, to our future here... I could definitely get behind Kyle Renado." He paused, a mischievous glint in his eyes. "And honestly, Grace Renado sounds pretty formidable, too. Especially when you're back to kicking ass."

Appendix: 3

In a world transformed by a devastating global event, a resilient community has forged itself around the remarkable figure of David. At the age of forty-eight, David stands as the patriarch, a man defined by his extraordinary intellect, a compassionate heart, and an innate sense of leadership. Possessing an intelligence quotient exceeding 148 and a unique, almost prescient understanding of the world, David is an autistic, altruistic, witty, and affectionate leader whose dominance is softened by his profound care for those under his protection. His most extraordinary trait is an intuitive grasp of past experiences from a life lived before, a temporal knowledge that imbues him with unparalleled foresight and wisdom. This remarkable inheritance is passed genetically; his children exhibit enhanced intellectual capabilities, skills, and strength, while his grandchildren receive partial temporal enhancements, ensuring the future vitality of the community.

Central to David's world are his nine wives, each drawn to him by different facets of his complex personality. Tiffany, his first wife, a maternal and fit woman with expertise in animal husbandry and veterinary medicine, has known David since their early adulthood, attending prom with him. Her attraction to his leadership laid the foundation for their enduring bond. Jennifer, his second wife, also a high school acquaintance and prom date, brings a playful and bisexual energy to the family. Her horticultural and botanical skills are invaluable in managing the community's hydroponics, and she was instrumental in recruiting other wives. Attracted to David's dominance, she affectionately calls him "Master."

Summer, David's third wife, is a smart and empathetic pharmacist and former soldier, whose attraction to David's foresight and care also blossomed during their youth. Elena, David's fourth wife, a smart and provocative former soldier of mixed Asian and Navajo heritage, was drawn to David's intelligence, joining his family after divorcing her previous husband. These four women—Tiffany, Jennifer, Summer, and Elena—form the core of David's marital family, having known him for an extended period.

The family continued to expand with the integration of more wives. Taylor, David's fifth wife, a petite and caring nanny and former soldier, was one of his students, drawn to his encompassing personality. Nicole, his sixth wife, also a former student and soldier, possesses a sweet and trusting nature, captivated by David's profound wisdom. Jessica, David's seventh and favored wife, a petite, sassy, and sarcastic woman, shares a unique connection, having been in a relationship with him in a prior existence and dreaming of him for years before their reunion. She lovingly calls him "Daddy." Kayla, David's eighth wife, an organized and fair individual, also shares a past-life connection with him, having been drawn to his unwavering commitment. Lastly, Tanya, David's ninth wife, a sensual Thai-Korean esthetician, resonates with his dedication and empathy.

David's influence extends through his children, who inherit his exceptional abilities. Aidan, his son with Tiffany, is a mechanic and engineer who manages the community's daytime operations, exemplifying his father's industriousness. Aidan is married to Alissa, Elena's niece, and they have a young son, Tyler. Brian, David's son with Jennifer, is a tech expert and gardener, working on the night shift. He is married to Seo-Yeon, Tanya's sister, and they are parents to their infant child, Dillon.

Junior, another of David's sons with Jennifer, is a formidable combat leader, gunsmith, and vanguard, leading the night operations. He has several devoted wives—Emma, Olivia, and Riley—who were former military personnel, as well as a lively mistress, Callie, Emma's best friend. Lily, David's daughter with Summer, is a "daddy's girl" and an expert fighter and marksman, married to Josh, whose mother, Lynn, was David's ex-wife in his past life.

The younger generation also includes Grace and Seth, David's twins with Nicole. Grace, sweet, observant, and stealthy, is engaged to Kyle, Kayla's brother, a skilled gunsmith who helped train Junior. Seth, her twin, is a kind and observant scout, with plans to marry Bonnie, Eric's daughter. David's family also includes young children and grandchildren, such as Lucas, his infant son with Taylor, and Poppy, his infant daughter with Jessica, as well as Jake, a surrogate grandson from Marvin and Sara.

The community is further strengthened by a diverse array of individuals who have joined David's fold through rescue or shared purpose. Lynn, Josh's mother and David's former wife from his past life, joined the community to be near her son after David rescued her from a dangerous ambush. Her parents, Clarence and Margaret, were also rescued by David. Mark and Janet, a teacher, along with their daughters Beth and Lori, were brought into the community during a resource expedition.

Junior, taking after his father, has led numerous rescue missions, bringing in many new members who form the backbone of the night shift. These include Andrew, Andrew's girlfriend Susan, Caleb and his girlfriend Sophia, Darrel and his girlfriend Reagan, Kathy who works in childcare, Marvin and his girlfriend Sara, and Noah, a high-caliber sniper who married Mia, a traditional Mexican girl rescued by David and Noah from a perilous situation.

Beyond immediate family and those rescued, David's community includes loyal allies like Eric, Parker, and Scott, former Army Cavalry Scouts who were welcomed shortly after the global event. Eric, Bonnie's father, is now dating Lynn. Parker, married to Jill who assists with gardening, and Scott, married to Andrea a nurse, both contribute their skills to the collective well-being. Andrea and Scott's son, Mike, represents another generation growing within the safety of David's community.

This intricate web of relationships, bound by kinship, shared purpose, and David's extraordinary leadership, forms a thriving community. Each individual, with their unique skills and personalities, contributes to the collective survival and prosperity, creating a beacon of hope and resilience in a changed world, all centered around the remarkable patriarch, David.

www.ingramcontent.com/pod-product-compliance
Lightning Source LLC
Chambersburg PA
CBHW071504170626
46811CB00007B/2728